# wilhelm's world

a fly-eyed view of human life

Copyright © 2003 John J. Roberts

ISBN 1-59113-314-9

Published by John J. Roberts USA.

All rights reserved. No part of this publication may be reproduced, stored in a retrieval system, or transmitted in any form or by any means, electronic, mechanical, recording or otherwise, without the prior written permission of the author.

PRINTED IN THE UNITED STATES OF AMERICA

The characters and events in this book are fictitious. Any similarity to real persons, living or dead, is coincidental and not intended by the author.

Booklocker.com, Inc.
2003

# wilhelm's world

## a fly-eyed view of human life

### compiled by his host

### John J. Roberts

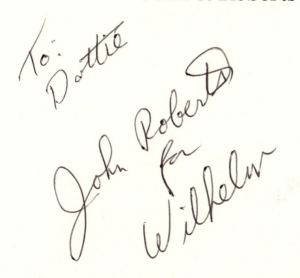

To: Dottie

John Roberts for Wilhelm

## Dedication

these writings are dedicated to dr. robert l. gallun, the scientist who made life miserable and/or impossible for billions of hessian flies while helping provide improved wheat varieties for the world. his career made my career necessary.

# Introduction

The diary-like entries collected here were discovered periodically over several years mysteriously stored on my home computer. They appeared intermittently on whichever diskette happened to be left in the computer. My first inclination was to simply erase them and blame them on some sort of glitch. However, since they continued to appear I finally decided to collect and save them to find out just what was really happening. I soon discovered that the writings were produced by a tiny Hessian fly named Wilhelm who laboriously dive-bombed the computer keys one at a time in order to provide the human race with a vastly different look at their world and the world of the Hessian fly.

Hessian flies have been and are a major pest of wheat in the United States and many of the wheat growing regions of the world. They earned the name Hessian fly, since it is commonly believed they were transported as pupae to the United States in the straw bedding of the Hessian soldiers' horses during the Revolutionary War.

Several state and federal research programs have been funded through the years to attempt to control the Hessian fly. The most noteworthy of these have featured the development and utilization of varieties which have genetic resistances incorporated through plant breeding techniques. The resourceful Hessian fly like many other crop pests has responded to these resistant varieties by changing its genetic makeup sufficiently to overcome these resistances. This has prompted a long war characterized by successive development and releases of resistant wheat varieties followed by adaptive genetic changes in the Hessian fly population. The human side of this war has been recorded at great lengths in the scientific literature, and should anyone wish to pursue this history, references are readily available upon request at libraries and the internet. The stories recorded by this tiny Hessian fly appear to be an effort to obtain some equal time coverage for their side of the battle.

At one point, it seemed that the literary Hessian fly would write forever. Sometimes, it would appear that Wilhelm had ceased to exist at all, with several weeks passing without any further tales. Then, an extended period passed during which there was no activity at all, so i decided to contact a publisher so the efforts of this tiny insect would not go unnoticed by the world. Shortly before the assembled works were prepared for submission, another episode appeared, explaining the long absence and suggesting that he had just begun to chronicle his fly-eyed view of the world.

## greetings

i believe i have just discovered a way to record my diary for the people of the world to read and thereby contribute significantly to the quality of history in general, thanks to the miracle of modern computer technology.  the owner of this computer is somewhat careless and leaves it on at least one night per week.  i have learned that i can write with this computer by flying to the ceiling and dive bombing the keys one by one, turning at the last second to land on my feet on the desired key.  this is a highly laborious task and does not allow me to produce capital letters or any other shift-dependent characters since it is quite impossible to depress the shift key and a letter key at the same time.  i can fly fast, but not that fast.  using the capital letter lock key is possible but adds too much effort to the operation.  the whole procedure is so difficult that it is probably a good thing the computer is only left on about one time per week.  it also tends to make me seek short words whenever possible.

## WILHELM'S WORLD

i will try to give you a slightly different view of the world. many things which seem so obvious from one point of view are considerably different when seen through the multi-faceted eyes of a .02 gram hessian fly. as a race of insects, we have been blessed with a rather fantastic type of genetic memory, allowing each of us to reach far back into the pages of our history as it is etched by the dna sequences on our chromosomes, and directly use the experience gained by those ancestors that passed their genetic codes to us. this compensates for the lack of written history that has been somewhat of a handicap up to now, but it appears that the advent of the home computer might just remedy that.

i think a bit of life history is in order by way of introduction to help you understand my type of life style. hessian flies were so named by you folks since you attribute the arrival of my ancestors to the straw bedding of the hessian soldiers horses during the american revolution. this is fairly close to the truth, but it was our intention to emigrate to america eventually so exploiting the transportation spawned by the revolution seemed to be the quickest way to get to the new world. it was not exactly a love boat type cruise and the recreational opportunities were totally lacking. we also quickly learned that the straw was not just for the horses' bedding. the next time we seek to colonize a continent, we will surely seek a better form of transportation. by the time the voyage ended, the straw was difficult to identify. when we arrived here, we were pleased to see this country had already begun large scale wheat farming, an activity critical to our survival. we must have wheat plants in order to complete our life cycle. we spend much of our lives as larvae and pupae quietly contemplating life and the meaning of the universe while securely lodged at the base of a wheat plant about an inch below the ground. from such a relaxing vantage point, it is easy to think clearly and not get sidetracked by activities of the day. the portion of our lives during which we are adult flies is spent in peaceful flight seeking a suitable mate and a hospitable wheat plant to serve as host for the eggs which will start the next generation of our race. unfortunately, we have not always been careful enough to control our populations adequately with the result that there have been instances in which our numbers were so great in wheat fields that the yields were drastically reduced. this served to rile the human population and led to some rather nasty encounters that i shall relate after my wings have had a chance to recover.

-ta, ta, wilhelm

## and salutations

here i am, back again at the old computer keyboard, wilhelm the hessian fly picking up roughly where i left off the other night. it is rather tiring to continue the aerobatics necessary to write with this thing, but i really should be happy that it works at all, thus giving me an opportunity to record my diary and relate to you some of the happenings and observations gleaned from several thousand generations of hessian flies in many parts of the world.

we have had our fate linked to the activities of humans for many hundreds of years since we live on wheat plants which you cultivate. throughout most of the early centuries of wheat culture man was pretty kind to us, being content to plant the same varieties of wheat year after year. these were very nice wheat varieties and served as super host plants for us for many centuries. we got careless and did not practice birth control, and our numbers grew so large that we began to do drastic damage to the wheat crop, reducing the yields substantially. this was a big mistake, and we attracted far too much attention, generating a rather severe backlash on the part of the humans. this led to the start of several major research programs to find resistance in wheat that would thwart our attempts to colonize the wheat plants. their efforts took several years, but were devastatingly successful and cost the lives of trillions and trillions of our compatriots. the resistant wheat looked just like any other kind, but was laced with genetic poisons that we could not detect until it was too late to turn back. the carnage was dreadful.

i have been elected to serve as chairfly of the human research committee and have been selected to live with or near people in order to observe humans to discover ways to get around their efforts to foil our lives. we have managed to develop some new races of flies with the ability to overcome the genes for resistance that they use, but they keep finding and using new ones all the time. i intend to study the habits of the humans in detail, and at the same time try to pass on to them an appreciation for our rich heritage so they will not be so intent upon our destruction. i was lucky to discover a household that not only has a computer complete with a handy word processing program, but also an owner who is careless enough to leave it turned on periodically, thus giving me an opportunity to record my messages for the world with some degree of regularity while they snore away.

    i have decided my first chore is to gain a thorough understanding of this human household before i try to delve into the intricate social structures which must exist in their cities and countries. this house is a good place to start so i will devote about an hour to a room by room survey flight in order to become familiar with my temporary surroundings. i must be rather careful since i look a little bit like an undernourished mosquito, a distant relative of mine but certainly not a friend. there is also a cat in the house. i have not seen it as yet, but there is a large cat outhouse box in the downstairs bathroom, just across the hall from the computer room. it would be just my luck to find that it is a real playful little devil with extra keen eyesight and i would get snuffed out by a quick paw swipe. to me, a cat is about the same relative size as an over stuffed, long haired elephant would be to a human.

    whew, that was a close one. i struck the period key a glancing blow, and slid down through the keyboard into the computer. it was very dark in there and real scary. i had to use all of my senses to find my way out without getting zapped like i see happen with those large bug zappers. had i been fried, i envision an archeologist thousands of years hence trying to figure what role the fossilized hessian fly had in the function of this primitive computer. i am glad i have not presented such a problem. i think i shall rest for a while and repair my jangled nerves.

-ta, ta, wilhelm

## tour de house

well, here i am again, ready to continue my orientation flights in this human home and relate tales of my glorious race of flies that dates back over one million generations. that is phenomenal when you consider that you humans have been in this country for only about ten generations and in the world as a distinct race for somewhere around two thousand generations. think how our race has developed history and culture through our many more cycles of learning.

i started to tell you of my tour of the house which is serving as my headquarters while i study humans. i hope to gain enough knowledge to help my race survive another million generations. you people seem intent upon eradicating us just because we choose to live on wheat plants and sometimes get carried away and do a little damage to your food supplies. from what i hear on the news, you often seem to be plagued by an oversupply of food, so i do not see why you should get so mad at us for trying to reduce you surplus grains a little bit.

    i had started to explore the house last time, when i had an accident with the computer and had to stop to rest and let my nerves repair.  we hessian flies have no drugs which we can use to calm our nerves so we rely on our ability to relax and soothe ourselves from within.  this house is rather strange, having most of the rooms you would expect, but it has two kitchens, and only one family.  unless the cat can cook, the extra kitchen seems silly.  the downstairs also has a bedroom, computer room, ping pong room, family room, and bathroom.  it seems to be furnished in a sort of mixture of mid depression and antique with a few modern items thrown in.

    i finally saw the cat.  it came downstairs and proceeded to chew on one of the plants in the family room.  i wonder if i should try to warn it that it might incur the wrath of humankind by harming the plants or let it find out the hard way.  that was a question, but i cannot get this thing to print a question mark easily since that requires use of the shift key, a feat beyond my capacities.  as i mentioned before, i can fly very fast, but not fast enough to hit the shift key and get back in time to activate the shifted function.  this cat is one of those fancy designer cats, a blue point siamese.  it is farther from home than i am.  it is not real old, but is not a kitten either.  i think i had better stay out of her range just in case it happens to be an insect hater by nature.  it just ran back upstairs so i think i will carefully fly up and survey things up there.  the cat has also chewed on the straw flowers in the living room, they are nearly ruined.  it will not last long in this house at this rate.

the kitchen upstairs is the most active looking, complete with a microwave oven and corning top range.  there are plenty of hiding places in the house so that if the humans ever come home while i am up and about, i should have little trouble finding a place of safety.  there are no signs of any insecticides around either, a good omen at least.  the upstairs is far more lived in and would seem to be the best place to avoid when the humans are home.  they just might mistake me for a mosquito and try to do me in.  there is a fly swatter on a nail behind the kitchen door so these are not the kind of people to be trusted in all matters.

i will rest again and continue the exploring tomorrow.  i hope i can figure our just how to turn the computer on by myself and not have to rely on the carelessness of the owner to make my writing possible.  i have learned how to save my efforts on the diskettes, but obviously cannot change them.  perhaps i can train the owner to collect them all together on a wilhelm disk for my convenience. that would be a big help. see you later.

-ta, ta, wilhelm

## hazards

hello again from wilhelm fly, hammering away once again on the old computer keyboard. i have finally completed the tour of the house. it was a very educational experience and my plan is to share it with the entire hessian fly population just as soon as i can figure out how to transmit the information. i will derive the formula necessary to convert from the computer to the frequency of the tiny antennae which all hessian flies have and use with great efficiency.

the trip through the house was not without grave danger, however. i used some rather poor judgement one time in selecting my flight path and my timing was off a bit too much. i got in front of the air return vent for the air conditioner just as it turned on, and got trapped and pinned helplessly against the filter. i was there for over ten minutes. luck must be on my side since no one was home at the time, and the cat did not notice my plight. the whole experience was extremely exhausting, both physically and mentally. i think that some sort of safety agency should post a suitable notice to warn of that particular hazard. perhaps osha will issue a flier to that effect.

    one of the most puzzling features of the human household that i am studying is the apparent fixation that humans have for items that really have no useful purpose. silly little knick knacks of all sorts of sizes and shapes are sitting in the way on nearly every flat surface in the house. i do not understand why the cat has not disposed of all of these things by now, since she seems intent on chewing all of the plant life in the house into extinction. she certainly seems to have a very destructive streak in her, but has managed to survive in this household far longer than i would have thought possible based upon her behavior. i am not sure that there is not some way for me to communicate with her. i will bet that she has some very interesting insights to pass on to the world and perhaps i can find a way to help her do so. i will search my vast store of genetic memory and see if i can dredge up some pertinent data on cats. if this computer had a functional modem, i bet i could tap some other sources of information. i think i shall try to plant a seed and get the owner to buy one. i could try to get back to the university since i know that there are many different data bases

# WILHELM'S WORLD

available over there, but i am afraid to try that trip again. i am far too small to attempt a flight much longer than a few hundred yards. even then, if it is at all windy, the odds are that i will never get to my destination. in order to get to this house, i stowed away in a briefcase over at the university. this seemed very safe, as what could possibly happen during a safe ride in an automobile with a staid old college professor. well, as i learned rapidly, a whole lot. in the first place, the old professor was not nearly as staid as i had guessed, and secondly, i should have stayed behind. he rides a motorcycle to the office. until you have spent 15 minutes inside a briefcase that is strapped to the rear of such a vehicle, a kawasaki spectre, as it zips here and yon, your life has been dull indeed. i must be the only gray-haired, white-tarsed hessian fly in the world. it was a terrifying ride and i will never again try to hitch a ride like that. next time, i shall try to find a much older professor to follow home. but then it would be just my luck to choose one that lives fifty miles away, and i would suffocate in his briefcase.

    i will now rest for a while, as i study the cat in detail, and try to find a way to talk to and with her.

-ta , ta, wilhelm

## riding high

hello again, this is your friendly hessian fly, wilhelm, back at the computer keyboard again after a somewhat prolonged absence due to a badly misaligned wing suffered when i got trapped against the furnace filter the other day. i think everything is okay now and i am back at full flight strength. during my recuperating period, i overheard a few things of great interest which i feel i must record for the benefit of the world in general. it seems you humans are really intent upon eventually wiping yourselves totally from the face of the earth. it will not be nuclear war or pollution or any of those other popular causes at all that do you all in, but rather your automobiles. it seems that it is obviously difficult enough to drive one of those complicated machines under the very best of circumstances without having some dire event occur. i have heard that over 50,000 persons per year are killed on your highways. personally, with that kind of record, i would definitely be inclined to find other places to drive and thus avoid the highways. to further complicate matters, many of you seem compelled to make the whole thing totally hopeless, by sending huge masses of drivers out to drive after they have been rather thoroughly dismembered by consuming great quantities of alcohol. this is particularly evident during one of your highly revered rituals called happy hour, during which you get two drinks for the price of one. i do not believe that you all do this voluntarily, but night after night, there you go, off down the road with senses so encumbered that it is small wonder that over half of the deaths and injuries on your highways are alcohol-related.

all of this brings me to the conversation i overheard a few days back. it seems your lawmakers, under considerable and, i must say sensible pressure, have begun to pass some pretty strict laws, state by state, that will finally deal harshly with the transgressions of the driver that has had too much to drink. i think this is a good start toward solving one of your major problems.

as happens so frequently when a new situation arises, there always seems to be someone with an idea designed to exploit it. i heard two people discussing the new laws, and they seem to have an idea they thought to be of great merit. it will be very risky for people to go out and drink now and then drive home or elsewhere.

people will still seek the company of others while they are imbibing since they do not want to become solitary drunks. the obvious solution put forth was to equip a large fleet of vacation motor homes with bars, bartenders, and non-drinking drivers. these traveling tap rooms could patrol certain areas of the city picking up customers on a scheduled route, much like the city busses. patrons could stay on for as many rounds and round trips as they wished, and then get off at the stop nearest their home and safely stagger home, posing little threat to the safety of others. these motor homes could be furnished to suit the neighborhoods in which they would ply their trade with plush furnishings and expensive, umbrella brandishing drinks for the rich neighborhoods, and beer and pretzels for others. these could also be equipped with small bands to cater to the crowd at hand and perhaps gather at certain parking lots to allow customers to change bars. this would be similar to tailgating, but every day and night, with or without football games, more like trailgating. there is a strong possibility that someone will franchise the whole operation and end up with a fleet of ginnebagos safely toting imbibers of martinis all over town with the satisfaction that many people are alive because they are now drinking and leaving the driving to us.

## WILHELM'S WORLD

hessian flies can sure overhear some strange conversations. talk to you later.

-ta, ta, wilhelm

## **tailgreating**

hello again from wilhelm, your friendly neighborhood hessian fly. it is good to be back at the old computer keyboard again after what has to have been one of the strangest weekends i have ever witnessed. it seems this was the first home college football game of the season. that in itself does not seem too strange, but you should have seen the strange activities this event generated. it is apparently a tribal ritual of some sort to prepare a feast of rather large portions to be consumed in the hot, sunny, dusty parking lot before the game to sort of demonstrate that all are in support of the institution and the event. i am sure that is much better than eating in the cool comfort of the air-conditioned home before leaving. at least it did get the gang out of the house early. they were certainly decked out in stranger than usual garb for the afternoon. they were also carrying radios and binoculars, probably to augment their somewhat weak hearing and seeing functions. after they left for

## WILHELM'S WORLD

the contest, i decided it was time for me to learn just what this strange behavior was all about.

i have learned to turn on one of the television sets upstairs since it has a remote control system similar to a computer keyboard. i easily found a football game which was just about to start, so i managed to see nearly the whole operation from the beginning. the cat heard the noise and came in to sleep on top of the set. nearly ninety degrees outside, and this cat has to sleep on top of a hot television set. i think she has been living with the humans too long and is getting weird from the association.

the coverage of the game began in the parking lot where several thousand people were eating, drinking, and standing around the backs of their cars. some were even cooking over small portable grills. although this was not the game to which my strange humans had gone, the announcer assured me that this same scene was being duplicated in the parking lots of hundreds of stadia all over the country. i learned later that this announcer was not an ex-player as are the majority who cover football games, hence the use of the unexpected but correct plural of stadium. i was fascinated to see this action and for a while thought that perhaps this was the major part of the football game. the people had special little tables that would fold and fit in the trunks of their cars. the cars were parked so each one could use some space behind it for their private picnic area. some people had simple repasts, consisting of fast food packages of burgers, chicken, artificial desserts, and soft drinks. in the mid-range, there were people with relatively fancy picnic lunches including home-fried chicken, all kinds of snacks and cheeses, and everything potable that was portable. several groups seemed to be competing to see which one could put together the most elaborate type of feast. they were using lace tablecloths, some with centerpieces, others even with candelabras, silverware, china, and one group even sported a three piece string ensemble. these types were even serving champagne in crystal glasses and imported beer, german, of course, in silver mugs. some of the vans had interiors which were much better than those found in many fine restaurants, complete with bars, refrigerators, and the ever popular and necessary bathroom.

the network covering the game even had a helicopter showing this vast parking lot with all of its feasting and revelry. as the time passed, the crowd began to get more and more animated and i thought the whole affair must be about to end. believe it or not, things were just beginning, and all of this eating and drinking in the hot, dusty parking lot was just a sort of preparation ritual for

# WILHELM'S WORLD

the football game that was just about to get started. the people all began to quickly fold up their tables and stash their goodies, and pack their trunks while they got themselves decked out in earphoned radios and necklaced with binoculars. they all then started into the huge battleground they call a stadium to witness the start of the real contest. i think i shall rest for a little while before trying to put the rest of the saturday happenings down in black and green.

-ta, ta, wilhelm

## the maim event

i am back again to continue to relate to you what seems to have been an impossible weekend experience. i managed to watch my humans take off for the first home football game of the season, and then watched the same sort of affair on television from some other part of the country. the first several minutes were devoted to the phenomenon called tailgating, definitely one of the strangest events any fly ever witnessed. was i ever surprised when the people left their cars and entered the large horseshoe-shaped battleground to continue with the activities. what a sight the inside of the stadium presented. there must have been over 70,000 humans packed in rows as if they were in a giant oval sardine can. in the middle of the whole mess there was a giant field of little bitty short grass with white lines painted on it. all this time, on television, there were very frequent breaks in the coverage during which the network tried to get the audience to buy everything from ale and beer to tires and vinyl siding. personally, with the heat and crowded conditions, i would think deodorant salesman might have gotten rich in a hurry.

all of a sudden it all got under way. humans with musical instruments and very hot looking uniforms poured out onto the field of grass and used the white lines to get lined up in what seemed to be a rather primitive imitation of a dot-matrix series of letters. the crowd yelled and then i saw the main reason for the noise. several young ladies who were definitely not in hot looking uniforms ran out on the field and began to spin some funny looking steel sticks in rough cadence. it was now obvious why the male humans had brought the binoculars, as all of them seemed to be in use now.

the band started to play one song and everyone in the whole stadium stood up and took off their hats while singing something that i could not make out. everyone cheered after they finished and sat back down while the band continued to play music you could almost make out over the din of the crowd. the whole place just kept getting louder and louder so i thought it must be just about over and sure enough, the band left the field.

boy, was i ever misled. i was just about ready to turn off the television set, which would waken the cat and liven up the rest of the afternoon, when more humans began to charge onto the field. i thought the band members had looked funny in their uniforms, but they were really pikers. there must have been nearly one hundred of them on each side of the field, wearing different colored uniforms, but each one had on a motorcycle helmet. there were a few on each side that were not in uniform and appeared to be administrative types. i guessed correctly from the outset of this new round of battle that these humans with the clipboards and headsets would be the true troublemakers in the whole affair.

all weekend, each event has seemed nearly too bizarre to believe, let alone relate in any sort of plausible fashion. now the really incredible part started. eleven members of each team lined up facing each other in the center of the grass field. everyone in the stadium stood up again while one man kicked that funny looking object you call a football to the far end of the field to the other bunch. at this point, major mayhem broke out and it is a wonder that there were not several deaths during the afternoon. that field was the scene of all sorts of aggression, fighting, deceit, penalties, and injuries. i learned a lot of the jargon that is peculiar to the sport but i think that i will have to study the game in much

## WILHELM'S WORLD

more detail before i really fully understand it. they talked about such things as offsides and illegal procedure a lot, but i did not see anything i thought was onsides or legal the whole time. and that reminds me, they had a huge clock at one end of the field, but it only ran part of the time. when they started the first quarter, it said that there were 15 minutes remaining. i kept track, and ten minutes later there were still 13 minutes and 24 seconds left. i hope someone fixes the clock before they play again in that stadium.

well, i watched until i became thoroughly and hopelessly confused. i shall just have to try again on monday night when i understand the older humans play for real and legitimate money. one thing was obvious during the game i have been watching, and that is that if just one of those guys had remembered to bring his motorcycle, it could have been real interesting.

-ta, ta, wilhelm

## cat tales

greetings once more. i have been spending quite a lot of time studying the cat that appears to own this house. whatever she wants, she manages to get and customarily expends essentially no energy whatsoever to get it. i have never seen such a successful creature in my life or in my inherited memory, so i think that i shall try to learn from her just how to extract such responses from the humans. if i can master that, i might be able to persuade them to stop spending so much of their collective energies to develop insect resistant wheat varieties.

    this cat is a blue point siamese type about 14 years old, clearly enough time to be in charge of all the areas she wishes to control. if she wants a window opened, she merely glares at it and meows softly and one of the humans proceeds to open it for her. after that, she generally wanders off to some other part of the house and ignores the elicited response while she briefly ponders her next command.  as i have mentioned before, she has an insatiable compulsion to chew on plants of all kinds, real or otherwise.  she has permission to travel anywhere in the house she wishes and does so.  she sleeps in the sun on the hottest days of the year as if she had no sense at all.  she exits the litter box as if she had been shot out of a cannon, often scattering litter several feet down the hall.  she seems to have a bit of a nervous stomach and regurgitates occasionally.   i am not sure that this is not an intentional type of behavior pattern designed to keep the humans constantly trying new kinds of food to stop the problem.

    i understand she suffers from some sort of prenatal shock that has affected her behavior with the television set.  when her mother was pregnant with her and the rest of her litter mates, she persisted in sleeping on top of the television set, even though the jump got to be quite a chore as she grew heavier with kitten.  after the litter was born, the mother was kept busy for a few days and could not get to the set.  when she finally did manage to extricate herself for a brief time, she trotted to the living room, crouched down and proceeded to jump way over the top of the set, having failed to allow for her recently lightened condition.  she did manage to look back as she sailed over it with a sort of chagrined look, since everyone knows that cats do not make mistakes. this seems to have had a major effect upon this cat. early in her life, she began sleeping on top of the nice warm television set. i do not think this is an altogether unusual behavior for cats. one night during a quiet program, she had slipped into a very deep sleep and fell from the top of the set to the table it was on, making a rather loud thunk in the process and opening herself to a large amount of humiliation. she has since repeated this in varying degrees and is lucky that she has not injured herself in some way. she is very self conscious about this embarrassing action and will often try to mask it by trying to make it look like she had intended to get down to get a drink or something.

    the humans now leave the rabbit ear antennae up on all of the sets in the house and small pillows where she is likely to land to offer her some protection. i really think she needs some sort of sleep belt to hold her safely in place as she sleeps. i wonder if this may be related to some of her other rather strange actions. i will have to try to find some answers to that if we can ever learn to exchange information effectively. maybe one of her falls jolted her brain or maybe even something important loose. i will have to think about this some more.

-ta, ta, wilhelm

## sports page

things have really been jumping around here for the last few weeks. it seems everyone is either getting ready to go to a football game or is gearing up to watch one on television. there are enough games broadcast during the weekend to more than occupy all of the spare time of everyone in the whole country. one channel even specializes in playing the same games over and over again, almost as if the object were to memorize them. they certainly try to make that possible for the better plays, showing them again and again via the instant replay. i was a bit perplexed by that system for a while, thinking that they managed somehow to get all of the players to reenact the key plays as a means of entertainment enhancement for the fans. i fail to understand how this race of humans finds time for all of their accomplishments. it should be easy for an industrious group of insects like my fellow hessian flies to stay far ahead of them in science and survive at will. somehow though, they still find time to develop new wheat varieties and thwart our efforts.  perhaps they learn something from all of their sporting events that aids them in their scientific endeavors.  i think i shall pay closer attention to these for a while.

the baseball season is nearing its close, according to the information i have gleaned.  they are in the midst of something called playoffs that seem to last nearly as long as does the regular season.  i obviously do not understand nearly enough about baseball.  the few times i have tried to watch it, i could barely stay awake.  they also tend to hit far too many fly balls for my comfort, and too many players fly out.  however, i am looking forward to seeing the whole world arrive  for the world series everyone keeps talking about.  perhaps i can learn about all of the other countries during that event.

now when football is on, there is little danger of falling asleep.  the people here get very animated during the games, yelling and screaming for many unpleasant things to happen to those they consider to be their adversaries.  it seems that they have a favorite no matter who is playing.  they must have gone to a lot of colleges and lived in many cities in order to cheer for so many of them.  it is also a little bit difficult to tell what part of the season that football is in at the moment.  the high school regular season is over, which means that there are only about four or five weeks left of playoffs to determine the state champions. the college season is about half over which means that they have not as yet determined which teams will be matched up in the various funny-named bowl games that are to be played for several weeks following the close of the official season. there is a lot of time spent in trying to decide which teams are the best each week, and several polls are issued to tell everyone about it. i think that they would be wise to let the teams figure that all out by themselves as the season goes on, and just issue one poll at the end of the year.

    the professional football teams are in the early part of their season, but to listen to the persons announcing the games, every single game is a pivotal one, crucial to the playoffs that will start in december. they are getting ready for a game in january called the super bowl, one which i can hardly wait to see. i have learned enough about the game in general now that i do feel a bit wrapped up in the spirit of it all. perhaps i might introduce some suitable version of the game to my fellow flies. the added dimension of flight that we enjoy would certainly make the whole game different. i can imagine some real fancy wingwork in some dazzling broken air scoring flights. passing would be far more difficult since all players would be able to intercept the ball. the single wing formation sounds a little bit frightening, however, triggering a mental image of a star player flying helplessly around in circles.

well, i think i will rest awhile and prepare for some more analyses of the human sports world. i understand that it is nearly time for basketball to start. with all of the other sports that exist, it must surely not be very important.

-ta, ta, wilhelm

## orderly chaos

once again i have overheard what has to be the strangest series of conversations the human world has ever generated. i have decided that humans are all a bit weird. when certain of the weirder types get together, it seems that their strange ways become exponentially exaggerated as their idiocy feeds one another. this was the case when i reported to you some time ago about the proposed venture to outfit vacation motor homes as bars and send them around town to pick up drinkers and keep them from driving while under the influence. these ginnebagos are probably just wild enough that someone will make a fortune with the scheme.

that was really tame compared to this latest in hair-brained human idiocy. the humans here were visited the other night after a football game by his brother and his family. the niece and nephew are about 16 and 14, and you would expect a bit of youthful silliness from them. there must be some type of reaction that stems from having this particular genetic group together, or as many are wont to say, redundantly, in close proximity, for, as the night wore on, it was difficult to tell who was the silliest of the bunch. they started a discussion about chemistry and physics that centered around the generally orderly sequences that are often found in nature and how that makes it easier to learn about them. several examples were given and then in some fashion, their thoughts turned to ways to make some of the other important parts of the natural world easier to learn and remember.

since it is often useful to use acronyms as an aid to learning, they decided that the names of the directions, although quite familiar to most, might be easier to learn if they spelled something besides nesw. so they picked a word of surprise and proceeded to name the directions george, oscar, sam, and henry. now there was not only a nice acronym, gosh, but the directions had been pleasantly personalized as well. there was some rather lively discussion about the effect of this change on some of the old sayings. moss will now grow on the george side of the tree, and young men will be advised to go henry and grow up with the country. some of the songs will require major rewriting efforts since the nature of the rhymes may be changed. other songs, however, will sound just fine, like oscar of the sun and henry of the moon, or george to alaska, or sam of the border.  there was a brief and heated exchange that centered upon the idea that there seemed to be too much masculinization involved with the selection of the names.  this argument waned as they started compiling a list of explorers and compared the relative frequency of male and female types.  as often happens, this logical approach was not very well received and the argument ceased.  since the main point of the whole exercise was to make it easier to learn the directions, and the proposal seemed to do just that, i thought they were now just about through for the night.

as is usually the case when i try to figure out what the humans are up to, i was wrong again.  they were just getting warmed up.  now they decided to make it easier to learn the calendar.  in a world which features the use of the alphabet to organize nearly everything, they decided to put the months of the year in proper alphabetical order.  in their silly system, the year would no longer begin with january, but would start with april.  all holidays would stay the same with the exception of new years day, which would now be the same as april fools' day, the two perhaps justly merged to cover the large throbbing heads of the over imbibers of the night before, september 30.  the new order of the months, and now truly an order, would be april, august, december, february, january, june, july, march, may, november, october, and september.  this would help make it easier for youngsters to learn the months and  would certainly be a refreshing change from the old patterns that have become so routine.  there will be several changes that might at first seem to be a little inconvenient, but surely not insurmountable for these super resilient humans.  the football schedules will have to be redone a bit, as will those for all other sports.  this in itself will take a lot of time.  if six weeks of winter follow the groundhog shadow sighting tradition, it will make for a really cold summer.  also, the first year or two the new system is used, there will be some substantial changes in the weather records for all months but june and july.  the christmas parade that is traditionally the sunday following  thanksgiving will now be a full five months before christmas, providing plenty of time to shop.  it will very likely not be cold and blustery for the parade honoring saint patrick, which will now fall in the old august timeslot, and those who are used to waiting until labor day weekend to close their lake cottages in michigan will find that mother nature will already have closed them for them.

    this whole thing just continued on and on, an explosion of silliness that seemed to have no limits.  i think they were just about

## WILHELM'S WORLD

ready to start on the days of the week next in order to have a truly organized calendar. i finally flew away to a quiet part of the house to let my weary antennae rest. the next thing you know, someone will decide to try to get this country to change to the metric system or some other equally absurd venture. my wings are about to drop off.

-ta, ta, wilhelm

## fly praise

hello again from wilhelm, busily at it once more from the keyboard of the friendly old computer. sometimes it seems that it would be more appropriate if i were a fruit fly writing on an apple rather than a hessian fly writing on a pc clone, but i think i had better not wait for someone to build a computer called a wheat.

i do feel a strong need to discuss what i think is a very grave situation that must be aired. recently, a high government official was forced to resign his position because of some comments he made in a news conference that were interpreted by some to be a blatant slur on certain minority members of society. a few years ago, i understand that another high government official, in a nearly private conversation, told a joke of questionable racial taste and subsequently resigned under fire. a general move throughout the country is growing to bring a halt to the use of ethnic jokes in order to try to keep from hurting the feelings of various groups. this concern for the welfare of others is admirable and does signify a move forward in the degree of civilization of the human race.

now i come to my real complaint, and i do feel compelled to try to generate some compassion for my position. i have heard over and over about the rights of the various minorities to be free from verbal attack, however well intended. the list of groups that can no longer be the butt of jokes has grown so long that i hear it finally includes the little morons that used to take hay to bed with them to feed their night mares and do other equally silly and mostly harmless things. it is even likely that the next minority group to secure protection from verbal abuse through demeaning jokes will be those high government officials who highlighted the problem in the first place. i am now going to make a plea for all humans to stop using insects, in particular the fly, as the means of describing distasteful events or items. a partial list of some of the glaring examples is difficult for me to relate, but it is necessary for the task at wing. fly-by-night as used to label a task of dubious merit or one whose likelihood of success is very low seems terribly unfair. since very few flies are nocturnal, the usage is not even very accurate. fly in the ointment is generally thought by humans to mean that something is wrong.  i would think that that could only improve the quality of the ointment and perhaps impair the efficiency of the fly.  fly off the handle is used to denote the act of being unable to keep a temper in check, but it is widely known that flies are extremely serene.  these are just a few of the phrases i think should be removed from use in human speech in the interest of promoting a deeper understanding of the flies of the world.

there are, after all, many types of flies which are of major importance to humans.  some are parasites of economically important pests of crops and livestock, helping to keep them in check without the use of pesticides.  even with this kind of effort, we can not even get so much as an honorable mention from the environmental protection agency when they pass out their annual awards.  the feathered buzzards get all kinds of accolades for their role in consuming dead critters.  were it not for various species of flies, humans would most certainly be up to their eyebrows in a diverse collection of carrion.  i think that for just a few of these good deeds, flies deserve to be treated with more respect.  it is highly possible that my species, the hessian fly, is really dedicated to helping the scientists of the world learn more about wheat.  were it not for our efforts, many of your modern wheat varieties would not exist since the need to develop them would not have occurred.

also, much of your current knowledge of the genetics of wheat was gleaned while studying our biological relationships with the wheat plant. surely we deserve some significant praise for this major contribution. the role of the fruit fly in advancing the frontiers of genetic research is also largely unheralded even in light of the many gene systems which have been explained through their efforts. the only flies that gain any press are those threatening citrus crops.

a news item recently pointed out just how insensitive some humans can be. it seems that a quantity of beef intended for the school lunch program was found to contain some insect fragments. all of the uproar this generated was that of chagrin over the possible damage which these fragments might cause. there was absolutely no evidence of concern for the fragmentees, who had lost their lives in the process. the worry about the effects of those little bits seems strange indeed coming from a population that eats such fragments as frog legs, chicken wings, calves liver and kidney pie.

oh well, now that i have spent the afternoon on my soapbox it is time to go upstairs and watch soap operas on television. i wonder how soap can sing. maybe it is because this is supposed to

JOHN J. ROBERTS

be the land of equal operatunity. i guess maybe even a fly should be pun ished for that.

-ta, ta, wilhelm

## **local series**

greetings once again from your friendly hessian fly, wilhelm, bringing you my fly-eyed view of the world through the magic of the computer keyboard.  and speaking of the world, that is really a very touchy subject with me right now.  you may remember that i was looking forward so very much to the baseball world series that i had arranged my schedule so i could watch it all and learn from the great spectacle that i anticipated it to be.  i envisioned all of the countries of the world to be in attendance, bringing with them their top people and accomplishments to display and impress the rest of the world.  this was to be the opportunity that i had really been waiting for since my duties as chairfly of the human research committee include the study of humans in great detail so that i can help our race of flies survive and prosper.  this includes the self-imposed charge to try to give to the humans information that will lead to an appreciation of our culture and rich heritage.  this has been made possible by the availability of the computer, whose word processing capacity and soft key touch are suitable to my style of writing.

    there i was, all ready to learn about the entire world in just a few evenings of television watching comfortably perched on top of an artificial mum safely out of sight of all but the cat. the cat has managed to demolish all of the real plants in the house, so only the plastic ones are left. the broadcast of the first game of the series began with an aerial view of the stadium, obviously very full of people who, i assumed, were from all of the countries of the world, a whole series of them. i had been led down the garden path once more since i soon found out the event that was starting was just another baseball game and that it was to be between two cities that are only about 400 miles apart. i sure do not consider that much of a world series as most of the world was not included at all.

    spectators were there from several parts of the country, a few other countries and some very strange looking characters who most certainly were not even from this world. as i have mentioned before, i am not terribly excited by baseball, but i did try to pay attention for some time. i hoped that the announcers would liven up the process somewhat, but i think that they, too, were having some difficulty keeping from drifting off. i did just that, and missed the bulk of the game. i think that a major part of the game hinges upon the ability of the participants with the largest stomachs to spit farther and more often than their opponents. it amazes me that in this sport, so much spitting occurs and is apparently expected. i wonder what the social reaction would be if the same behavior prevailed in your retail establishments with a clerk who spat as he helped you with a pair of shoes or a salesman with a large wad of tobacco generating a need for frequent expectorations tried to convince you he had just the television set you needed. i did find that i was looking forward to the breaks in the game, not really breaks in the action, so i could learn the latest in the available ways to earn a cold beer.

having finally decided this was not going to increase my knowledge of the human race appreciably, i have decided i shall concentrate next on another way to learn about the whole world. there have been many ads lately on television touting a coming special on country music so i am certain i will get an opportunity to at least hear songs characteristic of each country of the world. i hope this will make up for the disappointment of the so called world series.

so long for now, in the meantime i am trying to figure out just how one is supposed to have a good day since that is one of the most frequent orders i hear. i do not know how a day can be had at all, be it good, bad or indifferent. sometimes the language really confuses me.

-ta, ta, wilhelm

## nary a fat lady

greetings again from wilhelm. i have just managed to ruin about three afternoons watching daytime television to see what i can learn about soap operas. in the first place, i was misled again since i thought i was going to get a chance to soak up some culture and enjoy some fine music, even though i could not see any way that soap could really sing. my hypothesis was that it would be some sort of animated or cartoon approach to a presentation of some of the fine operas of the world. i was not really even very close as most of you know. animal and comic might come closer to the actual nature of the productions.

i was really quite embarrassed by much of what i saw so i suffered through three afternoons of them trying to figure out just what was going on. i never did see any soap of any kind throughout the entire ordeal, but judging from the language used by the participants, there were plenty of occasions that merited having the mouths of the performers washed out with soap. the plots were all about the same in each of the episodes i watched, essentially totally lacking. the characters most often represented some sort of beautiful person that had a spouse that was just about to become an ex-spouse for good reason. then followed a thorough mixing of spouses and ex-spouses until it was impossible to tell who was currently legally living with whom. not that legality seemed to matter in the least as it seems obvious that anything goes. i see why these are on in the afternoon while the kids are at school since the whole mess would be far too complicated for students to figure out, and besides, it would be too much like some sort of math or genetics problem to try to solve. the mating scheme did remind me a bit of a recurrent, reciprocal selection program such as is used in several kinds of plant breeding programs. on one of the series, i think that the starring actor had been married to or lived with at least three fourths of the cast of the program, and this did not include his real life activities. if the small cocktail lounge and the large bedroom were off limits for these programs, there would be left only an occasional scene in a hospital waiting room. this might not even change them much at all since the dialogue is just about the same regardless of the surroundings.  it is very interesting that no matter what time of day the players perform, they are always impeccably groomed and attired, unless, of course, they are in bed.  i wonder when they sleep, bathe or comb their hair.  such activities around here seem to occupy a goodly portion of the available time.  having seen how the humans look as they rise, i think it is good that they devote their morning energies to fixing the tosseled hair, removing whiskers and resurfacing faces and eyes.

this whole experience has managed to answer a lot of questions for me.  it is now obvious why so many people have regular jobs that require them to be away from home for much of the day.  the punishment for staying home is indeed very diabolical.  i am surprised that i lasted through three afternoons of the soapies.  it must be some sort of terrible ordeal to be faced with a long term sentence of them.  they are definitely a major component of what serves to keep the total productivity of this country very high.  my guess is that they are secretly produced and sponsored by the federal government as a ploy to keep the nation at work.

enough for now from the edge of the turning world or something to that effect. -ta, ta, wilhelm

## folktales

hello once more i am here to relate to you another of the many tales i have overheard from the folks who live here, hence the term, folktales. over the past few years i have managed to eavesdrop several times and gleaned much truly interesting information about some colorful characters that have been involved with their families. many of them defy description but there is one in particular that is definitely worthy of some extra effort.

it seems these folks were involved with the operation of a small poultry farm, raising turkeys to sell either live to a processor or dressed --that does seem like a strange term for an animal who is anything but dressed -- to a group of regular customers. these efforts required some extra help at times, and some real interesting characters were hired on a fairly regular basis to help with the operation during the busy times. the most memorable of these characters assured himself of his place in history through several highly distinctive actions.

many years ago this farm raised the broad-breasted bronze breed of turkey. they tended to be somewhat larger than the currently popular beltsville white breed, especially the toms. one afternoon just before the holiday you humans call thanksgiving, a young neighbor boy came over to buy a turkey. his mother said they wanted about a 25 pound bird. our character of characters proceeded to pick up his handy turkey hook, walked into the pen and caught a huge tom he had been trying to sell for a long time. he took it over to the scales and announced that it weighed 48 pounds. clearly this was too big so he released it and walked around in the milling birds and then proceeded to catch the giant cobbler once more. this time it once again weighed 48 pounds so he released it again. he repeated this routine several times always catching that same giant tom. he finally told the youngster that all of the turkeys must weigh 48 pounds so he would just have to buy a larger bird than he wanted. this worked fine until the boy got home and explained the dilemma to his mother. she was well aware of the shenanigans of our star character and managed to parley her giant bird into two reasonable sized turkeys. had this happened with a large male chicken, it would have been considered a rooster ruse. as it was, it was just typical tomfoolery.

since my wings are getting pretty tired i think i will save the rest of this characterization for later.

-ta, ta, wilhelm

## lastride

while i am recalling episodes i have overheard about the famous character who marketed turkeys with such skill, i will tell you another tale which is characteristic of this man. he did have a slight drinking problem and certainly enjoyed a nip now and then. he was particularly skillful in seeing that the nows and thens were always very close together. for example, after he and others had spent a long hard day dressing turkeys, the owner of the turkey business would bring them in the house to warm up for a few minutes, pay them for the day's work and provide a rewarding shot of whiskey. our prize character was exceptionally helpful during these events. he even went so far as to help pour the whiskey for the others. he did let the boss lady hand out the filled shot glasses to the others, and while her back was turned, he would manage to down his glass and refill it at least two and sometimes three times before she had a chance to turn around. if it has been a particularly rough day at the old turkey slaughter house, this routine would be repeated with the same results. none of the other workers ever ratted on our character. this was probably out of peer respect for his wily ways.

this love of drink had surfaced much earlier in our character's eventful life. his original intent had been to train to become an undertaker. that may be why he was so good at dressing turkeys and also what cultivated his love of liquids that had preserving qualities. after he had completed the formal schooling required by his state for this type of career, he had to serve for a year as an apprentice in an established funeral home in order to qualify for certification. he was lucky to be accepted by one of the most prestigious establishments in the area. he was so certain of his eventual success he proceeded to design and order promotional materials for his own business which he planned to open at the completion of his on-the-job training.

this funeral parlor had one very strange feature. many years before, an immigrant from germany known only as poppy stone died without any family, friends or information to enable him to be traced to anyone at all. this funeral home embalmed him as a sort of public service but then instead of the normal burial, they fitted his coffin with a glass lid. they kept poppy stone in the attic of the funeral home and allowed the ultra curious and stout of heart to view him to allow them to see the effects of embalming. although this seems a bit morbid, it serves to highlight the incredible range of curiosity which these humans have.

    now re-enter our star character. he was working at this funeral home diligently learning the applications of the schooling he had just completed much as apprentices would in any walk of life. one fine day our star had decided he had earned a few nips to reward him for the imminent completion of his training. the few nips increased substantially as our character continued his efforts. as he was moving some coffins in the attic, he spotted the coffin of poppy stone. he knew all about poppy and in his drink-elevated mood, he decided that death for poppy stone was pretty boring and that therefore he deserved a break. since it had been many years that poppy had been confined to the dreary attic, our character decided it was time poppy had an outing. he wheeled the glass-lidded coffin to the elevator and headed downstairs. he wheeled the coffin out on the deck and backed a hearse to it, loaded poppy into the vehicle and started off across town taking poppy for what he thought was a much-deserved ride. somehow he managed to convince himself that poppy not only enjoyed riding, but would like to go real fast. with this in mind, our hero proceeded to race through town at speeds far faster than were safe and definitely fast enough to attract the local law, who finally tracked him down when he had to stop and wait for a train. he explained to the officer that he was just taking poppy stone for a ride and could not see anything wrong with such a benevolent act. the officer was not impressed and neither was the licensing office responsible for his certification as an undertaker. he never got a chance to utilize his training but did manage to lead a very colorful life after all.

i questioned the truth of this tale for some time after i overheard it, thinking is was just one of those much-heralded urban legends. recently, i spotted a highly collectible shoe brush and mechanical pencil both of which bore our character's name as an ad for his never-opened funeral parlor. strange creatures these humans.

-ta, ta, wilhelm

## flying paper

stories certainly do abound around here.  i think the humans i live with must attract other humans whose lives have been blessed with rather bizarre events and/or characters.  whenever two or more humans gather together, a good bit of the time is eventually devoted to telling tales of one sort or another.  the other afternoon the neighbors came for a visit, some iced tea and general chit-chatting.  it was sunday and my humans were commenting on the great skill exhibited by their newspaper deliverer who somehow manages to carefully put the paper in the paperbox on those days when it is sunny and dry.  on rainy or snowy days, he lobs it onto the driveway often in a puddle, but always it will land with the open end of the plastic bag headed so that water can conveniently run in and thoroughly soak all but the classified advertisements.

thus was elicited a tale from their neighbor about his newspaper route escapade while growing up in texas. he was ten years old and not quite old enough to have his own paper route. one sunday he was asked to deliver papers for an older boy next door. his parents insisted on taking him in the car and helping him to complete his substitute task safely. they drove to the area and watched as he walked up to each of the designated doors and placed a neatly folded paper inside a screen door or other similar safe haven. this was an agonizingly slow process but was done with such meticulous care that it was very obvious that this lad was definitely not at all suited to be a full-fledged newspaper boy. he put none of the papers on any roofs, none in the buses, nor did he even manage to grind any front pages to shreds by sliding them across the concrete porches. he probably did not even look the part, since nary a dog chased or even barked at him.

finally the operation was completed and it was time to head for home and get ready for church. there were a few papers left over so our young paper prodigy asked his father if they needed them any longer. obviously, his father answered without thinking of the possible results of his reply and told him that they no longer needed them and would get rid of them. our young friend promptly gathered up all of the surplus papers in the back seat and proceeded to throw them out of the window of the car as it was tooling down the city street at thirty-five miles per hour. several other cars were tooling along as well, but one in particular was deeply involved in the action. the blowing, swirling papers were very effective in covering the windshield and thus completely blocked the vision of the driver. our paper pitcher looked back in time to see the newspapered car swerving frantically back and forth across the street and luckily get stopped before any real damage was done. the driver got out and rather forcefully peeled the papers from his windshield. he then started after our young paperboy and it soon became obvious that he wanted to have a chat with the persons responsible for the windshield-obscuring rainstorm of newspapers. the neighbor said it was not until he was in the armed services several years later that he again heard such language as was used by the highly irate motorist during his five-minute diatribe.

this was the only paper route experience for this young man. as soon as he was old enough for his own route, his father bought him a push lawnmower and a wagon to set him up with a lawn service, a really good choice since that driver might still have been out there somewhere.

-ta, ta, wilhelm

## ducks ahoy

humans seem to have so many strange habits involving needless and sometimes dangerous activities that it is remarkable that they have managed to survive at all. one of their more peculiar fetishes seems to go far back into the period of history during which it was necessary to hunt wild game in order to sustain life. currently, the most demanding hunting is for a parking place at the grocery store, a ritual often characterized by a person driving several times around the lot seeking a space as close to the door of the store as possible. this keeps them from having to walk an extra thirty feet so they will have enough energy conserved to jog two miles or play racquet ball for an hour after work.

even so, many modern nimrods don strange clothing, arm themselves with very expensive shotguns and rifles and take to the wilds in search of beast and fowl. the provender which results is generally only five or ten times as costly as similar fare would be in the convenient grocery store, but the sporting opportunity does prove to revitalize the avid hunter. based on the results of a bizarre hunting episode i recently overheard, it is not necessarily the game that is always in the greatest jeopardy.

two stalwart hunters embarked very early on a cool december morning in search of golden eye ducks. this is a diving duck that patrols relatively swift-flowing rivers seeking small fish as they float and dive their way downstream. one method of hunting them is to find a point on the upstream part of an island and wait in ambush for the ducks to float into range and then shoot them. this generally requires using chest waders to cross over to the island in river water that is often dotted with small pieces of ice. another more popular means is to quietly float the river in a canoe or similar conveyance and hope to overtake unsuspecting ducks when they surface before they can either dive again or fly away. the latter was the method of choice for our two hunters.

they departed at four in the morning in order to get their vehicles and the canoe in the proper places so they would have a way back to their starting point after their outing. it was just getting light and the temperature was a sultry 21 degrees fahrenheit as they launched the boat and started looking for game along the river. a cold front was passing through so they looked forward to a much cooler time as the day progressed. it was not a fit day for ducks either since after the first two hours of floating they had seen very few feathered creatures, none of whom had webbed feet. they were also the only hunters on the river and not only saw no one else. they heard absolutely no shooting, a pretty good indication that other hunters were having any luck or were safe and warm at home. the most exciting part of the outing up to that point was the light lunch and hot coffee, keeping them somewhat warm and a bit busy some of the time.

    boredom in this situation not only broke out but also led to some rather drastic results. in order to rest his cramped muscles the paddler in the back of the canoe quietly sat up on the edge of the canoe, thus giving his legs about one extra foot of space and allowing some blood to seep back into his feet and toes. this would seem to be a rather innocuous act but this time it certainly was not. as the boat rounded a slight bend in the river, the front paddler spotted a surfaced duck and very quickly fired at it. He missed the lucky bird but the canoe did not fare well at all. since the back passenger was sitting so high, the recoil force of the twelve gauge shotgun toppled the canoe over into the river, hunters, guns, food and all. they managed to struggle safely to shore but were really not safe at all considering the weather and their soaked condition. as they surveyed their situation they noted that the container with the rest of the food and coffee floated nicely, but slowly out of sight around the next bend, followed by the capsized canoe which also disappeared slowly down the river.

however, the immediate problem was to figure our how to avoid freezing to death in their soaked clothes at the below freezing temperatures. they were lucky enough to have dry matches and they quickly gathered dry leaves, twigs and anything dry enough to burn and built a fire to keep them warm and dry their clothes. this drying operation lasted for over an hour and they began to feel a bit better about the whole situation since now all they had to do was to walk out to a road and find help.

after they put the fire out and started off to safety they made a very distressing discovery. they were on a large island, separated from the mainland by at least 50 feet of very cold water. they had been so involved with handling their first dilemma that they had failed to check out the territory. they repeated their previous operation once more, this time on the river bank, building a fire and drying out all over again. then they trudged off to find a road and help.

one other mistake marred this adventure as if it had not already been sufficiently marred. some of the dry vines and limbs they selected for the drying fires turned out to be poison ivy. one of the two hunters ended up in the hospital due to the effects of being exposed to and inhaling the smoke. they did return later and retrieved their guns and later recovered the canoe. the featured characters in this tale of woe, both college professors, probably did not relate this adventure to any of the college classes they taught, particularly not the graduate level ones.

one of these fearless hunters had another type of rather bizarre experience recently during a deer hunting trip in a large hunting reserve in the southern part of the state. his day had been one of substantial frustration, sitting or walking for several hours in very cold, windy conditions with nary a sign of any antlered game. he finally decided to give up, get in his car and head home empty handed.

as he was driving out, he was just getting warm when a very large buck deer jumped the roadside fence on the right side, crossed in front of the car, then jumped the fence on the left side and slowly wandered off. the hapless hunter quickly grabbed his rifle, slammed the car door, climbed the fence, tearing his pants and started off in pursuit of his prey. he quickly caught up with the deer and lined up for a clear shot. his elation at the happy situation died when he heard the click when he pulled the trigger. he had forgotten that he had wisely emptied his rifle when he put it in the car.

he hurried back, climbed back over the fence, adding a new tear and hurried to the car to get ammunition. unfortunately, the car was locked and running and he could see his shells but not reach them. he was forced to break the window, then grabbed the shells, loaded his rifle and headed back across the fence, this time tearing a leg, and sought his trophy deer. it seems the wily deer knew that he was now actually in jeopardy so had exercised great judgement and left the area. now there was nothing left for the hunter to do but recross the fence, this time without major incident, and head for home in a very drafty automobile.

hunting certainly does require great strength of character and body. personally i think it would be fairer if the hunters had to catch their prey bare handed as their ancestors did in ancient times. it also makes me wonder if the hunted animals are able to plan their activities to extract a bit of revenge for the years of seeing their comrades killed. i think that both the golden eye and the deer planned their timely appearances to generate the maximum amount of trouble for the humans.

-ta, ta, wilhelm

## moving on

boy, i sure did overhear a real bombshell this time. just about the time i have gotten a bit used to the style of life and the weird climate around here, i find out that the whole household is about to pack up and move lock, stock and barrel to the fair state of georgia. i had been scrolling through some interesting correspondence dealing with a new wheat research position in georgia, but never guessed that it was intended for the old hoosier forever type that lives here. i got a hint of the possibility last week when he went to georgia for a quick visit. when he returned, there was a lot of talk about the trip, and then, the next thing i knew, they were talking in detail about arrangements to sell this house and move to georgia.

    they have already purchased a carrying cage to transport the cat. they call it a catabago, to avoid mentioning the word cage to the cat. the moment that she even so much as suspects that the door on that contraption will close, they will not get her near it with anything less than a log chain and winch. they might even consider keeping their house plants in it after she learns how it works. she certainly would never venture into it to bother them. i have heard the incredible racket this cat makes when she gets anywhere near the car. she howls at the top of her lungs from the minute she is carried to the garage and is still howling when they bring her back from a short trip to the veterinarian. i think she associates the automobile with examinations and injections. she is without doubt the worst automobile passenger in the world.

several discussions have concentrated on determining the best means for moving nearly everything in the house from the antiques to the tractor. there is just a bit of a problem as i see it at this juncture, however. so far, there has been no mention of any provisions for safely moving me. they must know by now of my presence as they do find traces of my writing fairly frequently and have arranged now and then to make my fly-writing even easier. i managed to get out here from the university by stowing away in a briefcase for what promised to be a quiet ride home with a staid old college professor. this turned out to be the first of many times that i made a major error in judging what the actions of humans could be. i ended up riding home inside a briefcase which was strapped to the luggage rack of a rather large and quick motorcycle.  i survived, but i am not sure i wish to subject myself to another white-tarsus ride like that and definitely not for a ride of over 600 miles.

    i probably will have to sort out my own means of transportation to georgia as i suspect that the humans here figure i am resourceful enough to do so.  were i to stay here, it would be my luck that the house would stay empty for a while and i would be immobilized by the low temperatures.  or, if it did sell quickly, there is little chance that the new owners would have a computer that i could use.  if the laws of murphy are working with their normal, awesome efficiency, this place would sell to someone with pet frogs, and my life would be snuffed out by a lightning-fast tongue.

    since staying here seems to be clearly out of the question, it is now my job to decide the best way to travel.  i am afraid that there is no chance that the cat will ride on the motorcycle in her catabago, although she might find that such a ride would be exhilarating at the very least.  the very thought of listening to her howl for about 650 miles is just about more than even the most stalwart and tolerant of hessian flies could stand.  the moving van itself is a possible alternative but there is no guarantee that i would not get lost somewhere along the way.  i think i will just find a suitable container that is going to be strapped to the motorcycle and sequester myself in it and brace myself for a stimulating ride to georgia.  there must be some of my genetic memory linked to a very distant set of relatives, the evil weevils.  they really liked motorcycles, the more exciting the better.

-ta, ta, wilhelm

## happy hoops

wow, another year has started already and i have not as yet gotten down to business. it is high time for me to really get down to business and begin seriously studying the human race and recording my observations with the help of this soft-keyed word processing computer. i have been a bit distracted lately, however. since the basketball season started, i have managed to spend hour after hour watching basketball games between nearly every organization imaginable. were i the same naive fly that started this assignment last fall, i would have been expecting some rather strange contests pitting tigers against bulldogs, blue demons against boilermakers or buckeyes against wildcats. there are indeed some pretty weird critters on the side of the floor. i saw a monstrous cardinal at one game that would surely put all the local birds to shame. i wonder what the bird feeders are like where he comes from.

i enjoyed football some, but although i had reservations about basketball, it turned out that it is really my sport. i am afraid that i am hopelessly addicted to it. after hiding upstairs during a few games and getting nearly deafened by the yells of the humans here, i discovered that the sports channel replays several games each day. i now can watch what i want when they are gone and do not have to hear them yell. if i could operate the video recorder i could study each contest in greater detail. i am sure a thorough understanding of this game is going to be an essential part of my human studying assignment. on any given day or night during the winter, there certainly must be more people involved in watching or participating in basketball than in any other enterprise. it is too bad that we flies are immobilized by the cold since we could do anything we wished to wheat during tourney times.

another major feature of this sport is that it allows women to participate and do more than merely cavort on the sidelines as is their cheerleading role in football. there still are the omnipresent spoil sports in the black and white striped shirts that insist upon blowing their whistles just when things get exciting.

i had my usual difficulty in learning the jargon associated with basketball, but it now really seems quite logical. a tipoff during which no one said a word seemed odd at first, as did a jump ball when the players jumped instead of the thrown ball. the first time i heard offensive foul mentioned, i expected to see some kind of ugly or dirty bird on the floor. not so. instead there was one of the striped-shirted types holding the back of his neck, frantically blowing his whistle and waving his other arm at a very innocent looking player. at this point some of the fans did seem to mention something about a weak-eyed turkey. what with dribbling, passing, backdoor buckets, slam dunks, blocks, picks, screens, free throws, one on one and fast breaks, it took some time to figure out just what was supposed to happen. now i am really hooked on the game. i have been trying to watch some of the games from the georgia area and think that it will be fun to follow basketball down there also.

of course all of this is only done to expand my knowledge of human behavior in order to aid the hessian flies of the world in our continuing battle for survival. i certainly would not watch merely for enjoyment, particularly not as many as five games per day on weekends.

my favorite play of all is the fast break alley oop which culminates in a spectacular slam dunk. i cannot imagine a terrestrial animal being able to master such a complex series of maneuvers requiring so much agility while floating through the air, but several teams have players that excel in this. it is always bound to get the crowd super hyped up, just as a missed lay up, blown stuff shot or air ball free throw will silence them.

i am looking forward to watching the harlem globetrotters soon since i gather that they will feature basketball with players from around the world and help me add to my store of information on humans. meantime i will study hard during the last part of the regular conference seasons.

come spring, i wonder if i will be able to entice any of my multitude of cousins into a game of horsefly.

-ta, ta, wilhelm

## **wordaholic**

i am back again, trying to work out some very perplexing riddles posed by this strange language these humans use, one that really is very confusing to me since hessian flies communicate in such a basically simple straight forward set of signals there is no chance to mistake meanings. i feel i must understand it properly in order to record my studies accurately. since we are on our way to a new life in georgia, i also think i should study the variances in speech i understand are practiced down there.

      one area of difficulty that is currently peopling me involves the function of the prefix re. it seems that i know many of the terms for which it is used in order to signify that a specific task is done again. for instance, rework means to work again just as reline means to line again. there are many other logical examples such as refinish, realign, relock, recharge, refill, remount, reload, repay, reopen, review, relive, and rethink. with these nice and neat words in mind, i was more than a little confused when i ran into the word revert and tried to find out how one verted. repeat did not mean to peat again at all. the entire system began to bog down for me at this point. i tried to find out just how to linquish something in the first place so it could be relinquished later. likewise, i do not know how to pell, vel, bel, ject, fract, flect, scind, semble, spond, sult, juvenate, dact, plete, tard, or dundant. this points out the fact that there is a series of words in which the base word to which the re is prefixed is essentially of no help at all in trying to define the word. to further complicate the system, there are several other words beginning with re that are characterized by having nearly no hint to their meaning contained in the base word. notable among these are record, revolt, reverse, retire, resent, remorse, require, repair, report, repast, reply, recur, request, respire, remain, relax, repress, retreat, and resign. it was pretty clear that red did not mean to d again nor that reap required repeated aping. i think i have figured out that these words must be treated by ignoring the re since it is not really a prefix at all in them.

    i guess it all boils down to a very straightforward system after all. there are several words in the language which, when preceded by the prefix re, mean to just repeat the function of the base word.  there are even more words, which, upon the prefixing of re, mean something totally different from the base word.  a still larger group of words exist that is seemingly prefixed by re, but upon removal of said prefix, a base word remains that is not a word at all.  there is also a smaller group of words in which the re is not a prefix at all, but merely serves to start the word since it must start with something.

i am beginning to wonder how, with such a system as this, humans manage to communicate at all.  perhaps i am about to discover the most promising characteristic of all about humans.  this revelation concerning the impossible nature of their language may be the weakest link in their chain of efforts to combat the pests of their food crop species.  as hessian flies, my race is ranked in that category by the humans.  i think that the efforts to exchange information about the means to control pests will eventually occupy more of their energies than will the actual duties associated with the research programs in laboratories, greenhouses and field nurseries.  i think that with that, i can now relax, review what i have learned, read, reread, and redact my writings and rely on this really remarkable computer to store it all for posterity.  after that, i shall get seriously down to the task of learning to understand the slight variances in the language which i understand i shall encounter in the south.

-ta, ta, wilhelm.

## dixie home

wow, that was certainly one of the most exhilarating experiences of my entire life. i just barely managed to stow away in a box of computer diskettes in time to have it taped shut and packed for the move to georgia. i learned the weather was too bad for the motorcycle trip and i was certain the computer materials would be among the very first items unpacked so i would be in little danger of ending up in a storage warehouse baked to a crisp in the georgia sun. i was just about right, he unpacked me pretty early, but his blasted motorcycle took precedence and he not only checked it out first, but i think he even took it out on a test run.

oh well, i am in pretty good shape considering that i have been cooped up for over four days and nine hundred miles in a moving van. the driver went from indiana to central georgia by way of the florida panhandle. even my limited knowledge of geography tells me that he must have been getting paid by the pound mile instead of the pound. i hope that the government does not find out that i was on board. that would probably generate more paperwork since i am classified as an agricultural pest, and we most certainly crossed several state lines, breaking many laws. i do not want this machine tied up with such bureaucratic folderol.

   i am now faced with learning about a new part of the country. since the climate here is much milder, i will have an opportunity to communicate with the local populations of hessian flies much sooner than would have been possible in indiana. i understand that they are still waging intermittent battles with a glacier up there, even this far into march. grass here is already in need of mowing and fishing and sunbathing seasons are already underway. it is obvious that there will be a lot of insect activity nearly all year long. this is my idea of heaven. it must indeed pay to be a clean living fly after all. the humans here must think the banana pudding the landlady brought today to welcome them to georgia is a part of heaven also to hear them talk about it.

   most of the arranging and unpacking is all over and things seem to be falling into a new routine. the cat is really fun to watch. she has not really learned her way around the house as yet, but is slowly establishing her special pathways. if she can go behind furniture she does, even if it means a longer trip. she may end up with a permanent crease in her side from the ledges in the window sills. she really likes to sun herself in them when the windows are open. she has been chattering at birds until her jaws must be nearly worn to a frazzle. there are many of them to watch and several new kinds to puzzle her. i hope i am present when she sees her first squirrel and her first deer. i understand she did see a large white muscovy duck at a motel in chattanooga on the way down here, but was so upset at her forced incarceration in her catabago that she refused to react to the duck at all.

    this house is quite a bit smaller than the one we left in indiana and is all on one level. the cat spent the first three days trying to find the stairway so she could go downstairs to hide. now she is beginning to feel at home and is not really hiding very much. a brand new feature of this house is the fireplace. it seems strange to me that with all of the efforts and education directed towards preventing fires, these humans actually plan to start a fire right here in their living room. i think i shall stay far away when they start playing with fire.

    one other new gadget in this house is rather interesting. up north, they ground their garbage up with a horribly noisy contraption and washed it down the drain. here, they have a trash geography tells me that he must have been getting paid by the pound mile instead of the pound. i hope that the government does not find out that i was on board. that would probably generate more paperwork since i am classified as an agricultural pest, and we most certainly crossed several state lines, breaking many laws. i do not want this machine tied up with such bureaucratic folderol.

i am now faced with learning about a new part of the country. since the climate here is much milder, i will have an opportunity to communicate with the local populations of hessian flies much sooner than would have been possible in indiana. i understand that they are still waging intermittent battles with a glacier up there, even this far into march. grass here is already in need of mowing and fishing and sunbathing seasons are already underway. it is obvious that there will be a lot of insect activity nearly all year long. this is my idea of heaven. it must indeed pay to be a clean living fly after all. the humans here must think the banana pudding the landlady brought today to welcome them to georgia is a part of heaven also to hear them talk about it.

most of the arranging and unpacking is all over and things seem to be falling into a new routine. the cat is really fun to watch. she has not really learned her way around the house as yet, but is slowly establishing her special pathways. if she can go behind

## WILHELM'S WORLD

furniture she does, even if it means a longer trip. she may end up with a permanent crease in her side from the ledges in the window sills. she really likes to sun herself in them when the windows are open. she has been chattering at birds until her jaws must be nearly worn to a frazzle. there are many of them to watch and several new kinds to puzzle her. i hope i am present when she sees her first squirrel and her first deer. i understand she did see a large white muscovy duck at a motel in chattanooga on the way down here, but was so upset at her forced incarceration in her catabago that she refused to react to the duck at all.

    this house is quite a bit smaller than the one we left in indiana and is all on one level. the cat spent the first three days trying to find the stairway so she could go downstairs to hide. now she is beginning to feel at home and is not really hiding very much. a brand new feature of this house is the fireplace. it seems strange to me that with all of the efforts and education directed towards preventing fires, these humans actually plan to start a fire right here in their living room. i think i shall stay far away when they start playing with fire.

    one other new gadget in this house is rather interesting. up north, they ground their garbage up with a horribly noisy contraption and washed it down the drain. here, they have a trash compactor they use to compress trash and take the mashed up mess to the local fire station when they get a large enough block to make the trip worthwhile. somehow, the fact that humans would spend a whole lot of money and effort on a machine to make little, compact trash out of big, bulky trash does not surprise me in the least. i think i am finally beginning to understand these humans after only about eight months of study. that really worries me more than just a little bit. i bet if one could invent an in-fireplace trash incinerator with artificial hickory smell it would be worth a bundle.

oh well, it is time to go watch the cat again. there is no telling what she might do next.

-ta, ta, wilhelm

## **willy-nilly**

life in the sunny south has certainly generated many new experiences for me as well as for the humans. mowing the lawn on new year's day was definitely a first for the man of the yard. i am sure he rarely even saw the grass in january up north, let alone need to cut it. he has also learned much about trees and sawmills and the real important task of standing around and talking. i think he has decided to become a bonafide expert at that skill. anytime an automobile hood is raised, it draws a crowd of three or four locals to comment on the situation and offer what may sometimes be constructive advice. usually one person wields some sort of tool while the rest become instant experts providing sage advice in what should be done with the tool in order to wrecktify the problem.

i heard some discussion by the landlord the other day that it was time to buy a pig to feed out in order to produce some real good country style meat.  at first i thought it would be fun to see what the cat would do with a pig, but then i discovered that a suitable enclosure was to be constructed outdoors to serve as a temporary house for the doomed beast.  although it was rather stylish when finished, it did seem like a lot of unnecessary effort for what was beginning to look like it was surely going to be some very expensive meat.

the landlord visited a friend who lived nearby who had several young pigs, picked out a promising specimen that suited him and paid for it.  he told him he would be back to pick it up as soon as the housing project was completed.  the pig supplier used a bit of the pig money to purchase what some refer to as white lightening, although unrelated to any weather phenomenon, and thoroughly tested it for quality.  when it was time to pick up the pig a few days later, the moonshine had managed to put the poor man in such a sound sleep that he could not be roused.  since they were there with a truck and had the help and advice necessary to load the pig, i learned that they decided  to go ahead and get the pig.  it had been raining for a few days, making the pig lot very messy, and they could not get to the previously picked pig.  with true southern resourcefulness they selected a suitable alternate that was near the gate, loaded it in the truck and brought it back to his new quarters. willy, as he was officially christened, was now a neighbor albeit a temporary resident.

a few days later the landlord got a call from the pig supplier's son suggesting that he should get over there quickly and get his pig since someone had stolen one of the others the other day. he carefully pointed out that the one the landlord had paid for was still there, but once pig rustling gets started, it can get pretty bad. predictably, honesty prevailed and the landlord explained what had happened and convinced the caller that a major crime wave had not broken out. i think everyone but willy the pig was relieved.

the next few months were devoted to the fattening process and the rather lengthy preparations for the ritual slaughtering and dressing of the hapless future ham. fortunately for my sensitive nature, all of these functions took place after it was far too cold for me to be outside so i was spared the gory details. the net result of the whole operation was that each person involved in the care, feeding and dressing of willy received about two pounds of pork, valued at only about thirty-five dollars per pound. they sure found a way to beat those high prices at the grocery store.

-ta, ta, wilhelm

## name game

hello again from wilhelm, back at the old computer keyboard again to try to keep my reporting activities current. it seems that there must have been another one of those super silly sessions in which several members of this family get together and see just how absurd they can be. on former occasions, they did such things as rename the directions, alphabetize the calendar, and tried to start a national wood chucking contest. the latest of their silly endeavors took just a few seconds of their time but will take me a lot longer to relate than the whole thing is worth, but i am pledged to record all of my observations of human behavior in order to aid my fellow hessian flies.

during a recent visit to the home of the older brother, a lengthy discussion ensued concerning the use of scientific names to facilitate uniformity in naming and discussing living organisms.

this has apparently been of great help in the science and research communities of the world, enabling persons of any country to refer to an organism with a high likelihood that other scientists will recognize what they did it to, if not what they did to it. latin was selected as the universal language to be used to identify subject organisms in published documents. these names are written in a set format and underlined to highlight their importance. unfortunately, since i can neither underline nor find the secret to producing italics, i will be unable to accurately depict the format, but try to imagine the latin sounding words that follow having proper underlines.

there are many familiar examples of latin binomials to identify various creatures. homo sapiens or humans have named nearly everything that walks, swims, runs, flies, grows, reproduces or otherwise calls attention to itself. hessian flies are dubbed mayetiola destructor, a title which i feel is unacceptable due to the inference that we are destructive. felis domesticus in no way describes the cat that lives here and occasionally charges down the hall at top speed growling like a wild beast.

the discussion of the merits of such a universal system of nomenclature led these crazy humans to propose developing a new field of taxonomy dedicated to providing universal names for inanimate objects. they suggested assigning latin binomial names to all objects, from armchair to xylophone. were such accepted throughout the world, they hypothesized it would be possible to communicate effectively no matter where you were. i think that a rather lengthy publication is planned, and will be titled an international guide to the scientific taxonomy of inanimate objects. as i learn of these i shall try to record them since they may someday prove to be of value to my studies of humans.

for some strange reason, the first item to attract their attention was a large glass-topped coffee table. it was duly christened tablum nonopaqum. the telephone in now referred to as perpetualus interuptus. the television set is the absurdius monoculatum while the radio is the ubiquitus hypervolumatum. the television remote control is the sposius aggravatium. the printer is the electradotus matriatum and receives its fodder from the electrabacus spp. the automobile seems to be one of the most difficult to name properly since there are nearly endless types of them. the genus decided upon was homotransportius with species names assigned to try to be as descriptive as possible. h. microbius is a sub compact car while h. miniroomius is a compact. h. mediocritus and h. elegantius refer to regular and large sized cars, respectively. one universal category seems to be reserved for any car that is plagued with far too frequent repair shop visits, namely h. lemonius.

i think i shall rest my weary wings now and let the computer cool off for the night. the computarius clonium shall be my name for this contraption.

-ta ta, wilhelm

## hayride

well, here i am again, continuing my diary after a rather embarrassing time spent away from the computer. i am now way behind in my writing, thanks to my own stupidity. i have gotten fairly bold in my visits in the area since the winds down here are not very violent and i have had a lot of luck finding my way back to headquarters. early last fall i was chatting with some local flies about their highly successful colonization of the wheat crop in the southeastern part of the country. i should have noticed that the area we were in was a field of cut hay, nearly ready for baling. actually, it was ready, since without warning, a huge baler came along and before i could say bermuda grass, i was firmly packed in the center of a large round bale. i could not even wiggle. the only bright spot i found in the whole situation was that at least i had company. several other hessian flies were trapped nearby so we could pass the time by visiting with one another. it must have been a bit like sitting around the campfire for about five months. we managed to discuss every topic known to flykind whenever we were warm enough to be active. several times it got so cold that we were a bit concerned about our chances for survival. fortunately, the bermuda grass served to insulate us from the severe cold and saved us from freezing to death.

    late in february, my bale was loaded onto a big pickup trick and hauled to a small feedlot. when the twine was cut, i figured that my troubles were finally over. complacency in my life generally precedes disaster or so it would seem. just as i was stretching my wings and preparing to head for home, the sprig of grass i had selected for a runway began to disappear into the huge mouth of a monstrous hereford cow, nearly taking me with it. i started flying in blind panic and managed to escape that cow and almost flew into the mouth of another one. i realized that cows are not carnivorous, but they would not have noticed me either by size or taste. i finally flew high enough to get out of the active feeding area and relayed warnings to my fellow flies who were just beginning to be liberated by the munching mooers. when all was calm once again, i began to collect my wits and started home thankful that i had not been smashed, frozen, or digested. i have since heard several people discuss the joys of wintering in

## WILHELM'S WORLD

bermuda, but i certainly think i can find a better place to spend my winters from now on. i think i have just spent the first leaf of absence by a hessian fly, sort of a haybattical leave.

-ta ta, wilhelm

## marksmanslip

a major part of my time learning about the ways of humans is spent viewing television when the household is left to me and the cat. many of the offerings are movies that are certainly neither first run nor even walk. several of these have been westerns that go back to the days of the singing cowboys. these have been a lot of fun to watch and have taught me quite a bit about changes in humans over the past several years.

    early westerns usually had common story lines which included bad guys, normally in black hats, who stole various items and threatened pure hearted ladies, and good guys who made everything all better with the aid of a trusty six-gun and a tireless horse. he could handle the six-gun with moves that were like magic. he could draw it with lightening speed and fire with uncanny accuracy. his horse was always faster than all other

## WILHELM'S WORLD

horses in the movie and never had to eat, drink, sleep or perform any of the normal bodily functions common to other animals. it would behoove owners of horse and buggy tour businesses in big cities to seek out the descendents of those screen horses to help keep the streets clean and save a bundle on feed. this would significantly lower the overhead and eliminate the underfoot.

starring cowboys were also excused from any of the normal life functions that would take time away from doing good deeds. they never soiled their clothes or their persons and could fight several desperados at once without losing their snow white stetson or getting their boots dusty. they were phenomenal shooters. they never missed a badman and never hit an innocent bystander by accident. should such appear to occur, it would quickly be revealed that the victim was, after all, a black hat type badly in need of being dispatched, and the shot was really carefully planned. they must have found time to practice a lot since they could hit nearly anything no matter what the range or conditions. if they ever happened to get hit by a ricocheting bullet themselves, it resulted in a mere flesh wound and was only a minor inconvenience, generating some tender attention from a tassel-skirted cowgirl.

the black-hatted bad guys were always treated fairly by these western knights to the point of allowing them the first swing in a fist fight and a clean head start in gunfights. the hero was often able to provide important morality lessons to the viewing public about the woes certain to befall those who broke the law. my favorite comment of all was from a western movie in which a wounded outlaw was complaining about the rough treatment he was receiving from the marshall. played by my very favorite, the duke, john wayne. the simple and effective reply was--if you don't like the treatment, don't rob the banks. seems pretty logical, even for humans.

this type of movie has helped document a major change in mankind through the years. gradually i have noticed that during a gun battle, the good guys are no longer very likely to hit the bad guy with the first shot. there has been a slow but steady deterioration in the marksmanship of the stars playing cowboys and law enforcement officers to the point that it is indeed rare to see an entire regiment of black-hatted bad guys bite the dust before a smoking colt. modern western warfare is much more likely to feature a shootout in which an extended exchange of targetless bullets leads to a surrender and an apology by the wrongdoer. the balance of the film often takes place in the courtroom with verbal battles and unappealing inaction.

    the good guys today include only a few old west cowboy types but mostly big city policemen and some modern day texas rangers.  they often   call in reinforcements which surround the crook and quickly force him to   surrender and begin extensive therapy.  the old white-hatted cowboy never had to rely on backup units to bring his opponents to their just desserts, his trusty hawgleg was the only help he needed.  even the highly trained modern movie policemen waste a lot of bullets and rarely hit anyone but bystanders when they are engaged in a pitched battle with gangsters.

    this all seems to me to indicate that the human race has gradually lost the ability to shoot straight and effectively control the criminal element.  i am confident that this will detract from his ability to effectively deal with other species he feels are his enemies, such as our race, the hessian flies.  perhaps if we can just hold our own for another fifty years of movies, the war will be ours indeed.

time now to take another nap. either these movies are making me sleepy or there was a tsetse fly in the strawpile somewhere in my ancestry.

-ta ta., wilhelm

## more cat tales

time to get back to work and catch up on the many confusing happenings here in humansville. i have been watching the cat for a long time now just wondering what she might do next to entertain me. she does a good job most of the time. she falls off the top of the television set in the living room about one night per week. her humans have placed a large pillow on the floor behind the set as a safety net to protect her aging bones. i wish there were some way i could record the sheepish look on her face when she crawls out from under the set. she knows that cats never make mistakes and is probably trying to convince us she just doing this to test the level of concern her humans have for her well being.

    a few weeks ago she really tested the system. she sleeps in window sills much of the time, moving somewhat like a sunflower to take advantage of the best sun angle. nobody in this household does windows so they hired a cleaning service to wash them and do some other heavy cleaning. they managed to get the windows nice and clean, but left one of the screens loose at the bottom. sure enough, the cat found the loose screen but unfortunately it was while she was fast asleep. she must have wakened when she landed on the pine straw next to the shrubs. the screen snapped back in place and this home-alone, totally indoor bound cat was locked out in the cruel, cruel outdoor world all by herself. she has not spent more than two minutes outside during her entire life and would have no idea how to survive. she likely thought that the outdoors was just a room that was much larger than the rest of the rooms she had seen with the walls all placed on the wrong side and furnished in a funny way.

luck has always been with this cat and certainly was on this day. the male human had forgotten some item for work and stopped by the house to get it on his way out of town. the cat was calmly sitting beside the drive as he drove up just waiting for someone to take care of her. as soon as the door was opened, in she scampered safe as could be, none the worse for her adventure. this creature is certainly about as successful as any could possibly be. i shall have to think about trying to emulate some aspects of

# WILHELM'S WORLD

her behavior to keep the humans from being so intent upon the destruction of my race.

    time to rest up again.

-ta ta., wilhelm

## swatch out

i am finding i am not alone in my difficulty in understanding the english language. the male human here is either very slow or very stubborn, i am not sure which. i may learn a lot about the ways humans try to communicate if i just pay attention to the pair that the cat lets live here.

    they are traveling to a retirement banquet up north soon to help honor several research scientists that are finally hanging up their microscopes and calculators and leaving the pest populations alone. the female human came home the other day with a swatch of brightly colored material which she had just dropped off with her friendly local dressmaker. the strong sales point for this action was that the new dress would absolutely go with everything, a characteristic which was obviously intended to highlight the frugality and sensibility of the purchase and the subsequent arrangement to have the dress made.  that seemed sort of logical to me also since males use a similar logic base, no matter what the species.

the human male and i quickly learned that we were far from the truth.  it was now her intent to buy everything to go with it since it would go with everything.  she clutched the swatch of material firmly in her hand and rushed from store to store buying belts, purses, shoes, hats and jewelry all of which matched the swatch perfectly.  she managed to acquire nearly every clothing item and accessory that could match the dress and then some.  i hope for his sake that the dress and the swatch are indeed alike and do match all of the everythings that she has assembled.  i am certain the total cost of the matching items is only about ten times the amount invested in the dress.  he probably got off fairly easy if i judge the average household correctly.

i am sure glad that the cat and i have perfectly coordinated outfits.  i hate to shop and do not have a budget sufficiently large to sustain such an endeavor as the one i just witnessed.  i guess i could look for three pairs of wing-tipped shoes.  they would match nicely.

-ta, ta., wilhelm

## upgrade fever

well, i feel i must record a part of the human behavior that really puzzles me.  when i started recording my observations the computer i used was an apple 2 plus, very easy to use and it had a nice soft key touch, a feature that is highly important due to the kind of fly writing i do.  it used two floppy disk drives for its main storage and although somewhat slow, it was quite adequate for my needs, as well as for the humans.  the entire word processing program fit on one of the floppy disks and the machine had a total memory of about 64,000 bytes, which sounds like a typical summer evening in minnesota.

the human here got a new computer at work that was almost ibm compatible so he could not use his home computer system to complement his work needs.  actually, i think he had better games at work.  thus started the upgrade parade here.  he soon brought home a new ibm clone that had a hard disk with 20 megs of storage space and the motherboard ram memory was 64k. it could perform several thousand computations per second, obviously several thousand more than the human could possibly understand or utilize even given much more time. the speed of access and computation was measured in milliseconds. the speed of the operator is likely measured in mega minutes.

as expected, his work computer was upgraded to a fast 386 with well over 200 megs of hard drive storage and a super vga monitor. now instead of watching words on the screen in blue and white, he could watch them in super blue and white -- a remarkable improvement.

once the work computer was well established, it quickly became obvious that the home system was quickly drifting into obsolescence and unable to properly complement the system at work. so we now prepared for the expected response. sure enough, he came home with a super fast 386 with over 300 megs of hard drive space, an enhanced, super vga monitor and a mouse that i cannot use, even if i fly into it from the side. it also has a fax/modem to allow him to communicate with the rest of the world if he ever learns how to use it.

the new home system was nearly three weeks old when the work system underwent a major upgrade epidemic, likely generated by a need to spend year-end funds. this would pose a substantial challenge to his home budget since he was now faced with a major state of the art system. i am certain, however, that as soon as i master the vagaries of this home system he will find a way to surpass it with a new super system. i have already had to learn three separate word processing programs and, of course, each new system has a different way to save and recall files.

so far it seems that he has managed to progress from a computer that operated at a speed that was about 15 times faster than he could think or react to one that is about 15000 times faster than he is. the major change i have noted during all these upgrades is that he now spends a lot more time staring at the screen in super vga wonderment while he tries to figure out what just happened and what he should do next.

progress is really wonderful around here.

-ta, ta, wilhelm

## **automania**

back again to try to sort out some of the many tales i have overheard that deal with the strange happenings with humans and their automobiles. cars are very often the dominant topic of conversation at nearly any gathering. stories concerning their role in life indeed range from the ridiculous to the very ridiculous.

many years ago a relative of the residents here attended a stag type party at a friend's lake cottage. as is the case today, the partying folk drank a bit too much and when they left to return to town, it sounds as if no one of the group was in any shape to drive. in those days, cars were much slower, roads rougher, traffic much lighter and the frequency of highway fatalities much lower. it is a good thing because when these marginally functional party goers turned on up the main street they spied a car double-parked in front of a store. one of the passengers noted this flagrant transgression and said they were obviously obligated to do something about it. another suggested that they must do something that would teach the wrongdoer a lesson he would not soon forget. the third passenger awakened from his booze snooze and suggested they just hit the s-o-b. that would certainly teach him. the driver liked that option so he did just that. he hit the parked car.

the lesson really started at about that time since the local law arrested them and hauled them to the city court building and summoned the magistrate, a man whose demeanor was little improved by getting called out in the wee hours. demeanors deteriorated even further as parents were called to come get their wayward offspring. when our driver's father arrived, the driver had fallen asleep leaning against the courtroom railing. i think that even though he was old enough to drive, he was still young enough to eat while standing for a few days.

it seems that driving and drinking sometimes go hand in hand much to the endangerment of the population. one of the local characters bought a small motor home a few years ago and found it to be a pretty good party home suited to small gatherings which allowed the cocktail hour to be celebrated on the way to one of their favorite local and regional restaurants and after dinner drinks on the way home. this usually meant only a short drive on rather quiet roads so fortunately no problems marred these illegal but highly enjoyable outings.

    this system worked well as long as two or more people were involved. one day our character found himself driving down the highway all alone. he realized he was getting pretty thirsty but did not want to stop and retrieve a cold beer from the refrigerator in the back of the motor home. the road was straight and flat so our resourceful hero started to figure a way to satisfy his thirst and not lose any time in the process. he proceeded to let go of the steering wheel and then kept track of the time the vehicle stayed on the road in a straight line. after several of these trials, he calculated that he could turn loose of the wheel, walk quickly to the refrigerator and return with a cold beer and have a two second margin of safety.

    i understand that he managed to pull this off without incident, unless, of course, you count the minor accident which befell the driver of the car he met while he was absent. this hapless man was understandably shocked to see the driverless vehicle and very lucky that the shoulder of the road was wide and firm enough to keep him from suffering a major accident.

humans spend so much time in their automobiles you would certainly think they would develop exceptional skills in the care and handling of them. the basic operation is really not too complex, but when added to the mistakes of thousands of other drivers, the permutations for possible errors are overwhelming. it is of great interest, however, to note how often very simple skills are completely lacking in the driving human. for instance, one afternoon a few years ago, our resident hero received a call from his wife's office mate asking him to come down and unlock the car for her since she had locked the keys in it. he suggested he would stop by on his way home after work. she said that was not a good idea since the car would probably run out of gasoline before then since the car was not only locked, but the engine was running.

another incident indicates a possible genetic connection coding for automobile difficulties. a cousin of hers was attending a meeting at the university, about a 45 mile drive from her home. she had driven her brand new cadillac and parked it safely in a covered parking garage. after the meeting, she went to her car and found to her horror the doors were locked and the keys were in the ignition. she called several friends who offered various solutions ranging from hammers to tow trucks. she finally called the dealer from whom she had purchased the car who went from home down to his office and looked up her key number. he called the dealer at home in the university town, who called a local locksmith, also at home, who then went to his shop and made the needed key for the shiny new, locked caddy. he took the key over to the distraught lady who led him to her car. as he started to unlock the car he made a rather disturbing discovery and reached in through the wide open window and handed the owner her keys. he did mention that in the future she might check her car more carefully before starting such an elaborate sequence of rescue events.

windows figured in another event i recently overheard. it seems that tobacco chewing generates a rather vile product in the form of ugly brown puddles deposited by the chewers. while discussing this habit my host related an experience years ago when he worked in a gas station. this was in the days of service stations when attendants went out to the car, asked how they could help and proceeded to pump gasoline, check oil, check tire pressure and clean the windows. one chewing customer nearly always managed to deposit a spittle puddle right outside of his window when he drove up, making it difficult to provide service without stepping in the disgusting effluent. once when the customer had gone into the station a flurry of extra service erupted and our hero washed all of the windows, including the driver's side which he rolled up to allow for meticulous cleaning. he must have cleaned it real good, since the first thing the customer did when he returned was to spit a large mouthful of brown juice on the inside of the window. this super nasty mess did provide a lesson of sufficient graphic content to stop future nasty pools of brown slop.

-ta, ta, wilhelm

## tis the flight before christmas

ho, ho, ho. this is the very first ever christmas letter from a hessian fly. those that are into collectibles just might seriously think about having this one hermetically sealed and laminated as it is certain to become incredibly valuable in the future. there are a few good reasons for this being the first ever christmas letter from a hessian fly. first, this is clearly the first time in history that a hessian fly has had access to a means through which the flown word could be translated into the written word. the soft keypad of this computer and my perseverance in dive bombing each letter key individually have made this all possible.

those who know little or nothing of the life cycle of the hessian fly would not know that generally we are in a state of deep hibernation in our pupa forms during the winter and have thus missed christmas for nearly two thousand years, hence another reason for this landmark accomplishment. this year since i am in the nice warm confines of a human house, i am able to experience this interesting holiday for the first time and record my feelings for the chronicles of flydom.

there has been a lot of activity around here ever since the family returned from thanksgiving with their brother in indianapolis. that holiday, characterized by massive bouts of overeating, apparently signals the start of preparations for christmas. over the past few weeks several strange things have happened. red and green decorations have replaced all of the other weird knick-knacks sitting around on all of the flat surfaces in the house. this has served to keep the cat a bit off balance as she has had to taste everything to find out which are the most chewable. i think she has finally decided to just chew everything regardless of quality. she knocks the small red sleigh on the floor about three nights a week, and tuesday she blatantly stood on the end table and chewed on the straw flowers in plain sight of her people. i will never understand how she has managed to survive for over fifteen years. periodically packages are brought in and covered with brightly colored paper and string. it is a strange ritual to say the least.

two fairly new phrases have been introduced to my vocabulary this season. bah, humbug seems to be the password of the male of the house. charge it seems to be the favorite phrase and activity of the female. i must admit that it would be easy to get caught up in the spirit of the whole thing, particularly if you listened to her.

it was pretty noisy the other night so when things had quieted down for the evening, i went into the living room to see what had transpired. believe it or not, there was a tree in there. it is some kind of conifer, but has really strange looking metal roots and the strangest fruit assortment that i have ever seen. most of it is metal or glass and not any of it looks like it is edible or that it would produce any kind of germinable seeds. after dark i was very surprised to discover that some of the strange fruit even has lights in it. as might be expected, this addition to the living room was a real challenge to the cat. she prowled around it each night and managed to dislodge several of the objects, thereby giving the humans something to do during the day.

all of these strange things that i have been witnessing i am just dying to pass along to all my relatives but there are some major difficulties which will keep me from doing so. first, i will need 42 billion copies of this letter and i do not think there is quite that much paper in the house.  also, all of my relatives are sound asleep at the base of their wheat plants this time of the year and would not see this letter until spring.  i am afraid i could not deliver them by myself either since the cold would bring me to a thudding halt very quickly.  i will just have to trust the world to deliver the first ever merry christmas from wilhelm the hessian fly by word of mouth.  whenever you pass a wheat field on your travels, just shout merry christmas out the window.  if you are on a plane, train or bus, you might do it quietly.  hope your new year is good, too.

-ta, ta, wilhelm

## new life

wow. Not only a new computer, but also a new word processing program with a feature that automatically capitalizes as needed if i could only figure out how to activate it. this will make my flywriting look like most other writers' efforts, but alas, it would remove one of my trademarks, the lack of capital letters, a feature generated by the difficulty i have in dive bombing the computer keys one-by-one to produce the record of my observations.

my life with these humans has been more than a bit confusing. it started in indiana and I was convinced that would be my home for many years. as soon as i was comfortable with that long range plan, he was transferred to georgia. it was very easy for me to adjust to the softer climate which enabled me to explore a bit more and meet some of the local hessian flies to glean information from them for inclusion in my records. stability of a high order seemed to have set in as they bought a nice house and proceeded to steadily improve and upgrade it. she suggested a series of minor projects which, as expected by him, rapidly expanded in difficulty, complexity and cost to consume his energy, brain power and bank account. to escape the myriad of indoor projects, he launched several outdoor ones of sufficiently urgent caliber to keep him out of the house for extended periods.

    his first and strangest project was to remove three stumps left when the dying pine trees had to be cut. fortunately he hired a professional to drop the trees, a very smart move based on what I have observed of his forestry skills. most stumps in this area are removed by a professional service in which the stumps are ground down to ground level by a large, noisy machine leaving only a pile of sawdust. our outdoors hero was not about to pay for that type of service, particularly in light of the fact that much of the stump remained under the surface and would eventually rot leaving a soft, low spot. his approach was very logical to him and he proceeded to remove the stumps using a combination of digging and cutting until he had the stump loosened from its roots. he started with the biggest stump which he considered to be the major challenge. every night after work he would don old clothes, take his shovel, saw and ax and proceed to dig a moat around the objective to provide access to the roots. this took much longer than he thought but he did provide much entertainment for the neighbors. each of them would stop by on their way home to see the current level of progress. all were great cheerleaders but opted not to interfere with his project. several weeks later he had managed to sever all of the roots using only the three tools mentioned. he now had the first stump free and ready to remove. unfortunately, he had a new problem. the pine tree had been about three feet in diameter, he had unearthed nearly four feet of stump and root stubs to yield a rather unwieldy and very heavy chunk of pine that he could not budge. a friend arrived with a wrecker, looped a chain around the huge stump and lifted it out of the ground and drove off into the sunset with the stump twisting slowly behind the truck. filling the new hole occupied several more evenings and then a similar effort followed to remove the other two stumps. they were much easier and also much less entertaining. thus ended the first of his major adventures but surely would not be the last.

his next outdoor project was to take care of the cedar siding on the house. he had congratulated himself on selecting a house that did not need to be painted and thus saving himself about three days of hard work every few years. as he studied the operation he discovered that like most things, this job was destined to be far more complicated that he thought. thanks to a very helpful neighbor he had access to a new and powerful gasoline-powered pressure washer. what power. he soon discovered that water at super velocity will instantly shred cedar siding, pop caulking from windows, bounce back in a full-face flush and travel without significantly reduced speed through a screen and soak the guest bed while terrifying the cat. the real highlight was when he modified an old cliché to read madder than a wet hornet. he sure came down his ladder in record time and luckily the dousing slowed the speed of the maddened stingers. he also learned that dripping and puddling water can significantly soften the ground around a ladder leg to provide a pulse-quickening sideways slide. all of these adventures happened during the cleaning of the first half of the front of the house. a few more minor mishaps occurred as he splashed his way around the house. the neighbors that had watched the stump project checked often to see what manner of entertaining antics would accompany his latest chore.

they were well entertained again as they watched him climb up the ladder, realize he had forgotten the cleaning wand, go back down and get it, clean about ten square feet of siding and then climb back down and move the ladder about three feet. he managed to make about three trips all the way around the house

## WILHELM'S WORLD

before he managed to complete the process. now he was ready to start the next step in his maintenance regime.

    i think i shall rest my weary wings before continuing.

-ta, ta, wilhelm.

## cedar tales

back to the house maintenance saga which had already exceeded by over a week the time he would have spent in routine painting. he had learned from other homeowners that he needed to rewash the house with a type of clorox compound to retard fungus growth. as if the ladder had not already made enough trips around the house, our hero now began to treat the house with a clorox solution which he had luckily thought to dilute and thus avoid bleaching the house white. he used the aforementioned pressure washer, wisely remembering to change the power setting to low. he then circled the house once again, treating the cedar siding, some shrubs and any wandering fauna that happened by.

the next step involved using a preserving compound to protect the wood from deterioration, as if he had not already done sufficient damage with his inept ministrations. his friendly consultants explained that he should use a sprayer to apply the chemical as that was the best and fastest method. the first gallon of preservative covered only a few square feet of cedar, several square yards on the ground via runoff and a few feet of overhang so he quickly calculated that at that rate, he would need about 75 gallons to do the whole house. at this juncture he switched to a three inch paint brush to continue the job, no matter how long it would take. this operation was not only slow but prompted the curious neighbors to stop on the way home and come to the house in order to see what he was up and down to this time. it is very lucky that he is in georgia since the same project in indiana would not fit between the last spring snow and the first one of the fall. the ladder could only be moved an arm's length at a time so i am sure he set a record for number of ladder moves to complete a job. he finally finished the job and, surprisingly, before it was time to start the whole thing over.

    all of this activity has nearly worn me out.

-ta, ta, wilhelm,

## more cedar tales

i was looking forward to some quiet times after the cedar activities but was wrong again. a new flurry of activity erupted in the back yard. he was clearing the brush and small trees from an area as if he was getting ready to plant a garden. judging from his speed in other things, i figured there would be fresh produce in three to five years. several sessions with saws, clippers, shovels and rakes produced a relatively level, rectangular plot about 18 by 25 feet but obviously not prepared for planting. i soon learned that this was a far different project. he was launching a very ambitious and, based on his skill level, probably impossible task. he planned to build a 14 by 20 foot workshop and have it match the a-frame shape of the central part of the house. also he would side it with cedar to match the house and give him some more siding to clean and treat. this first part of the operation he called site preparation and involved many trips to the back yard to measure, position stakes, deploy string and then move everything and start over.  his helpful neighbor noted a need and supplied a transit to enable accurate placement of stakes and strings, hopefully before the cleared area reforested and presented him with more stumps to remove.  remarkably, he mastered use of this instrument in only about ten hours and finished the first trial layout.  there then ensued a rather lengthy period during which the properly-positioned stakes and string slowly deteriorated while he tried to figure out his next step.  he realized that the string would not be enough to hold the concrete in place so he borrowed some metal forms from his technician.  after several attempts, he managed to get them in place.  then the next period began and in order to get his forms back before they became a permanent fixture. his technician ordered the concrete and arranged to get it delivered, poured and finished.  now the site featured a brand new pad to serve as the floor and foundation of his new building.

the next era in this project lasted nearly three years.  it was called pad curing and was not really based on his professionally polished procrastination skills but on a report he had read stating that lengthy curing times added significantly to the quality and strength of concrete.  he was satisfied that his pad was cured perfectly and could withstand truck and bus traffic without damage.

i think a bit of rest is in order before continuing with the project description.

-ta, ta, wilhelm

## materials and equipment

it finally seemed that building could begin at any time, provided the proper push could be directed towards our hero.  the super helpful neighbor surfaced once more and suggested that some building materials would be helpful should he wish to actually construct something.  fortunately, he did not dare suggest that he plant some trees of suitable types to provide lumber for the project or this would be the world's longest diary entry.  he did have a friend at work who was in the process of clearing some land and sawing several trees into framing-sized boards.  he went down and helped stack the boards and found another opportunity for creative procrastination.  now he had to wait for the wood to cure.  a few months later it was time to take the cured boards to a wood treatment center.  i thought they were already cured so i was a bit puzzled by this part of the operation.  perhaps they had had a relapse. as always, a slight hitch cropped up to cause another delay. he now had to borrow a truck and trailer of sufficient power and size to haul the boards. once more his technician came though and had the right combination to get the job done. the chore now centered around getting this large truck and the attached trailer to the wood source, load it and take it to the treatment facility. the truck was rather more complex than any vehicle he had driven. he first learned that the wiring was hooked up properly but the lights did not take directions well. he not only had no reliable turn signals but also had no brake lights. the brakes were not very good anyway so he just drove very slowly and always kept his eyes peeled for a soft, cheap item to hit in the event of an emergency. his real challenge arose when he needed to back the trailer to the stack of wood. no matter how hard he tried, the trailer would not go the way he wanted it to. i learned that jackknife is not only an item commonly carried in a pocket, but is also a swearword-generating maneuver which forced repeated efforts to get the trailer to go straight back to the wood. the law of averages finally prevailed and he managed to get the rig positioned to load. to his chagrin, he learned that it would take at least two trips to move all the lumber.

he muddled through these tasks, again waited for the treating phase, and then borrowed the rig again to haul the lumber home.  the neighbors were treated to another show as he tried to back the trailer into his driveway to unload.  it took him several tries to get the rig far enough into the driveway so the truck was not blocking the street.  fortunately he did not try to back all the way around the house to the backyard.  now began the great wood shuttle part of the project.  he picked up each board and carried it to the pad and stacked them in neat piles.  the wood was pretty heavy due to the liquid used for the treatment.  after he had successfully stacked all of the framing wood, he started a very important phase of the entire program.  it was obvious that he would need some special equipment in order to proceed with his construction project.

i could not believe the next flurry of activity.  i had always thought his wife was the shopper in the family, but now it was obvious that his unpaired x-chromosome had some latent genetic tendencies directing him to shop with a vengeance.  he bought three power saws, a table model, a chop/mitre saw and a skill saw.  i assume the skill resided in the saw since i am sure it is well hidden in him, if present at all.  further forays resulted in nails, screws, roofing materials, measuring tapes, levels and a truckload of cedar siding. he tried to wrangle a laser level out of the deal, but the two hundred dollar price got rather firmly vetoed by the chief bean counter. after he set up all of these new toys on the pad, he realized he had no power out there to operate them. thus started another chapter. he has always been a fan of underground utilities so he decided to dig a ditch from the power source at the house to the construction site.

his friendly neighbor pitched in once more after noting that three weeks of digging by hand had resulted in a ditch that was only about five feet long, with about 95 feet to go. so he could see the project finished before he retired, the neighbor supplied a tractor and ditch digger and finished the ditch in about thirty minutes. soon the slab was supplied with power and a telephone line, but the ever popular television cable was overlooked. had he included it, his dream shop would have been perfect. i think he is finally ready to start building. this should really be fun.

-ta, ta, wilhelm

## at last

this day should go down in history as one worthy of note. after only about five years, it seemed that an actual structure was about to become reality.  he now started his detailed plans for the framing stage, drawing each layer as he envisioned they would be installed. as he progressed, he added up the sizes and numbers of boards he would need. in spite of his complete lack of experience in construction, he managed to saw all of the boards to the proper specifications.  his stacking skills were not too good, however, since he ended with the boards he needed first on the bottom of a large stack. at least thanks to considerable drying time the boards were all a bit smaller and lighter weight than before and thus easier to handle. after restacking, he came to the realization that he now would have to actually learn how to build.

once more his neighbor came to the rescue since he knew that if he were to rely on our hero to actually get started, he would likely be too old and feeble to wield a hammer. he brought a box full of anchor bolts, a chalk line and several other necessary items. after laying out the pattern for the base plate, he demonstrated the technique for using the big drill to install the anchor bolts. this very powerful motor nearly turned the student into a propeller when he insisted on holding tightly to the drill after the drill bit got stuck. a few such events were sufficient to teach him how to use the drill. he soon had a building that was two inches high, probably much more progress than many had bet. the kibitzing neighbors checked the progress regularly to be sure they missed none of the entertainment.

    i was amazed to observe a steady flow of activity and true progress for the next few weeks. the compressor, power nailers, extension cords and free expertise certainly facilitated the operation and the building soon was nearly complete. as he started to furnish the inside of the building he made a major mistake. a local store had a sale on wireless intercom units and the bean counter figured it was a good deal so she bought it and gave it to him as a shed-warming present. had he been at all aware of the sanctity-busting nature of the present. he would have thought of a reason that it would not work inside the new building. now it was possible for her to directly interrupt his serious activities as he set up the inside of the new building to get it organized and properly furnished.

sometime after it appeared that the backyard projects were finished, a neighbor offered our resident contractor a huge stack of surplus bricks, free for the taking. another lesson followed as he learned that his small pickup truck could hold many more bricks than it could safely move. thus he gained some extra exercise as he loaded and unloaded several hundred bricks. after they were restacked in the backyard, he decided it was now time to derive some sort of plan for their use. his first brainstorm was to make a brick walkway from the house to the new out building. this was a real challenge since he now had to dig a shallow trench in which to place the bricks so they would be level with the ground and keep him from tripping over them and the lawnmower from chipping them. he followed the path of least resistance from the house to the new building, the freshly disturbed trail of the power and phone lines. he was a few bricks short of finishing the job so he had to buy more. when he finished the walkway he did realize that he had effectively sealed the buried lines and he had several extra bricks so he started another project, a brick patio just out side of the back porch. he managed to finish that project in record time for him and again had bricks left over so he built a brick apron for the new building and a brick structure in which to burn leaves.

he finally seemed to run out of ideas and space for brickwork. he calculated that the bricked over areas would save enough energy in lawn mower gasoline to pay for the bricks in only about 75 years.

it now seemed that they had all fixed up the way they wanted their house, yard and outback building. they could now sit back and enjoy their retirement years in relative comfort. once again i was deluded into thinking i could predict the actions of these strange people. they attended a fair in a nearby town and came home with a fist full of brochures and pamphlets. next they went to a show which featured all kinds of recreational vehicles. i had no idea what to expect next but was very surprised when i learned they planned to sell this house that they had so laboriously improved and maintained and buy some sort of weird home on wheels so they could travel throughout the country. this could be done without having to worry about leaving the cats home and bother with arranging for someone to care for the house while they traveled. i faced this big change with mixed emotions since i was relatively certain that it would generate a bunch of situations for

## WILHELM'S WORLD

which my hero human is highly unlikely to possess sufficient expertise to handle. also, this would provide me an opportunity to see much more of the world without any appreciable wing effort. thus, i am prepared for a whole new chapter in my life.

-ta, ta, wilhelm.

Printed in the United States
994600001B